PRAISE FOR ANDREA HURTT

"COLORFUL, DESCRIPTIVE, FASCINATINGLY PROVOCA-TIVE... Andrea Hurtt's *Masquerade,* is a WONDERFUL story about relationships and consequences. Just when you think you know what happens next, you realize THAT YOU DON'T! Not by a long shot, because that's what deception is... a mind trick that lets you think you've got it all figured out. At least until everything unravels. This is a FANTASTIC first novel and I can't wait to see what stories Andrea Hurtt weaves next."

— DEB WHITE- STAFF WRITER FOR *NERDS AND BEYOND*

"Maquerade keeps you intrigued from the very first sentence. The writing is so descriptive I felt like I was right there, and when it ended I felt like I lived it! I eagerly await Andrea's next book!"

— DOROTHY CHAMBERLAIN

"A thrilling tale that pulls you into Grace's world. The passion, fear and blame that Andrea takes you through on this journey are so real that I found myself biting my nails through the last chapters. I can't wait to read more of her books."

— LINDA STECKER

"For the bibliophile who is looking for their next addiction, you have uncovered the secret of Andrea Hurtt's '*Maquerade*'! This stand-out novel weaves a suspenseful tale of love, deceit, and the necessity of discovering ones own strength and self worth. Her mastery of the pen and attention to detail is a fresh infusion of talent to the literary world and I cannot wait for the next edition!"

— RIANNA MELTON

UNMISTAKABLE

RAZOR'S EDGE BOOK TWO

ANDREA HURTT

To my family -
Thank you for standing by me as I leapt into this crazy adventure.

To my friends -
Your support means so much more to me than you will ever know.

To Linda -
Thank you for giving me the "Hope" I needed to move forward with my dreams.

To BSB -
I couldn't ask for a better group of guys for my inspiration!

CHAPTER 1

It had been months since she'd heard from her best friend, Grace. Unfortunately, this was nothing new. Hope's dearest friend didn't reach out to her for months at a time.

Oh, the life of being an actor.

Not Hope.

She had a plain, boring, average office job.

Then the phone rang. She missed the call, but her phone dinged, alerting her to a voicemail.

Her heart skipped when she heard Grace's voice. "Hope! My theater troupe's doing a show in Spokane. I'll leave comp tickets at the Will-Call for you, if you can come."

A week later, she stood outside the back entrance of the theater, since they had a tradition after every show.

Some of the main cast would walk out to sign programs, and her friend would be out there.

Grace was so busy talking to an older gentleman that she jumped when Hope shoved a bouquet of daisies under her nose.

"I know you don't like flowers," she said. "But daisies have always been some you could enjoy." Her bestie lifted her gaze from the flowers and locked eyes with Hope.

They crushed the poor flowers when they embraced.

There were a few cast members that hadn't left yet, so Grace introduced her. She met Charles, who played Louis, the lead opposite Grace's role.

Despite that, he was shorter than her friend, the guy had a presence about him. His charisma was overwhelming.

Charles had dirty blonde hair that liked to stick out in every direction and intense brown eyes.

"Since Spokane is two-and-a-half hours away, I've got a room at a hotel close by. It has a nice bar in the lobby. Would you like to walk over to have a drink?" Hope asked. She didn't want to waste precious time with Grace standing outside the theater chatting.

"We've got one more show to do in town tomorrow night, so I've got to keep things short, but I would love to."

They ordered drinks, Hope a cocktail, and Grace ordered a soda.

"Since when do you miss out on a chance to have a libation?" she teased.

"During showtimes, I don't partake at all. Not until the show ends."

Hope forced a smile, sipping her rum and coke. It was obvious Grace was doing nothing but the theater with her life lately. She missed her so much.

"What's been happening in the good old South-West Wash? Anything changed in your life?" her friend asked.

Although the two of them had been apart for a few years, Hope would always consider Grace her best friend.

"I started a new job a few weeks ago. It's going well..."

After two drinks, Grace said she needed to head back to her own hotel.

The company had to be up early; they had a TV interview for the local news station.

Sadness swirled around in Hope's tummy. She didn't want to say goodbye already. They hadn't seen each other for so long and she feared it would be another long stretch. They hugged again and said their goodbyes.

It was another four weeks before there was any correspondence with her dear friend. She'd hoped that the little time they'd spent in Spokane would help keep them in touch.

When she heard nothing from Grace, she started getting worried. Hope reached out first with a quick email. Using her friend's childhood nickname, it encouraged her she'd hear back.

Hey Elvis,

I know you've been busy lately; I read online about you and the success of the show. But would it hurt to send a quick text message every once in a while, just to say hello?

The last time I saw you just wasn't long enough for us to rekindle our friendship. I hope you don't mind, but I'm planning on coming to your final two shows in L.A. I got things at work all figured out, so I could take the time off. I've already got my airline ticket, but I don't have a hotel booked. I'd like to stay somewhere close to you. Do you know what hotel the troupe is staying at? The sooner I find out the better, so I can get a room reserved before they're all gone. It is in two weeks, after all.

I 'hope' to hear from you soon!
Hope

She finally got a response about a week later. Sort of.

Hope stepped into the kitchen to grab a soda, and her phone rang. She couldn't get to it fast enough. The missed call told her it'd been Grace. She set her soda on the table and promptly called her friend back.

"Hewwo," the voice on the other line said.

"Gracie? Are you okay?"

"I'b gob a moub foo o reefe'f."

Her friend had candy in her mouth. *Reese's* to be exact.

When they'd done their first and only play together, they'd developed a need to have *Reese's Pieces* at every rehearsal and performance.

They should've gained three hundred pounds from all the candy they'd eaten.

"Ahh. That makes sense. Well, I won't keep you long. I just wanted to make sure you got my email; I haven't heard from you in a while." Hope heard her friend swallow.

"I called you to let you know I hadn't checked emails lately, and just found yours. But then it went to voicemail."

Hope giggled, and she couldn't stop. "We did it again," she said. "Calling each other at the same time, like we used to."

"Well, it's a good thing I took a moment to shove some candy in my mouth. And you don't have to keep it short. I'm sitting in the room all alone. Everyone else took off to go hit the slots."

They spent the next two hours talking. Hope's sides hurt from laughing so hard. They reminisced about the fun times they had, and the actors they'd had crushes on when they were teens, and a few they still did as adults.

They talked as if they'd never been apart.

Hope hated to let her friend go, but they both needed to get some sleep. After she hung up, she felt so much better. She needed to book a room at Grace's hotel for her upcoming trip.

A week later, her bestie called again.

"I totally forgot to tell you about the benefit ball! It's raising money for the theater. It's a masquerade, can you believe it? So you'll need to bring a ball gown and find a mask."

Hope had never had a reason to wear something so fancy and spent the remaining time before her trip to L.A. frantically looking for the right one.

When she finally stood outside the door to her friend's hotel room and saw what Grace was wearing, she felt like her dress choice had been spot on.

Grace's midnight blue dress fell to the floor, hiding her beautiful silver strappy heels.

Hope pulled her gown from the huge garment bag and her bestie gasped at the burgundy piece of art.

"Wow! That's stunning! And your ringlets are fitting! Chocolate brown, compliments the color of the gown! Dear Hope, you remind me of a character from my all-time favorite movie."

They grabbed their masks from the desk in the bedroom and assisted the other to get the elastic over their heads without damaging their hair.

Hope had a burgundy mask with gold trim around the edging and glitter sprinkled across it.

Her friend's mask was silver with matching trim around the edges and glitter filigree around the eyes. In the center was a diamond-shaped midnight-blue stone that held two matching blue ostrich feathers in place.

"Are you ready for this?" Grace asked. She grabbed Hope's hand and gave a gentle squeeze of reassurance, although she was terrified. She didn't do crowds or fancy events.

The elevator seemed to take forever to get them down just a few floors.

Hope smiled. "I think I should ask you that. You look a little nervous. It's just like walking out on stage. If you need to be someone else tonight, that's okay, too."

"I'm good. Let's do this!"

THE BALLROOM of the grand hotel was filled with women elegantly dressed in floor-length gowns, and men in stunning black tuxedos.

The décor was fascinating. It was as if they'd drenched the room in glitter.

A masked man came toward Grace and Hope.

"That's John, he plays my father in the musical." Grace pointed out.

Behind his mask, Hope saw a headful of shocking white hair, sticking in every direction. He reached for her friend's hand and Grace accepted it. "Ah, my beautiful daughter," John said. "And who is this divine creature you have here?"

"I'd like you to meet my childhood friend, Hope. Actually, we met doing a small community play together."

"Oh? Another actress in my presence?"

"No, not me," Hope said. "I'm content to be behind the scenes or in a seat."

John took her hand to graze her knuckles with a kiss. "Pity. You're as breathtaking as any diva I've ever seen on stage."

Hope felt the deep blush, sure it was visible through her mask. She'd never been good at taking a compliment.

"If you'll please excuse me," John said. "It's time for a drink."

"Should we go get something as well?" Hope asked after the older actor had left them.

Grace smiled at her. "If you'd like a drink, I'll go over there with you, but I can't have one for another forty-eight hours. I've been alcohol-free for almost five months. No drinking while doing shows. But Sunday, after the last show, hell yeah."

"Oh, right. I forgot."

"Please, have one! I insist. At least one of us should enjoy all the free liquor."

Hope sipped at her glass of champagne, glancing over at her friend. She watched Grace's face visibly pale, and she looked around for the cause.

Charles, her bestie's co-star, was headed their way.

He wasn't alone.

Two other masked men trailed behind him.

"Gracie, I want you to meet my brother, Nick, and his friend, Blaze," the man barked, not bothering to look her way.

Hope glanced at the brother.

Wow, he's tall. At least six feet.

At barely five feet and four inches, everyone was tall to her, though.

"You must be Grace. Charles has spoken of you often, and with such affection." The man's voice was soft, kind.

Hope's tummy flip-flopped. She could listen to him talk all night. So sexy.

He extended his hand to her best friend, and she couldn't tear her eyes away.

"May I have this dance?" Nick asked.

Charles stepped in between them. "*No.*" His voice was sharp. "You're up for auction. You can't dance with anyone until then."

Grace's features twinged, her brows furrowed slightly, and her cheeks heating red at the tone in her co-star's voice. No one else would've seen, it was so slight.

She knew her best friend well enough to know that hit a nerve.

Grace's response was sweet, like butter. "My apologies, but I must decline. I *am* up for auction, if you still want that dance. All the proceeds will help the children's theater."

Nick smiled again at Grace, sending jealous butterflies through Hope's abdomen.

"Well, then. See you at the auction," he said.

"If you'll please excuse me."

Before they moved, Hope didn't miss her best friend glancing at the other man.

He had black hair, and the mask he wore was black with blood-red trim.

Her eyes kept returning to the tall blond man.

Grace touched her arm, and she almost jumped.

"Let's move over that way. I should learn more about the auction, and I need to find out where you can be so you aren't standing alone while I go up there."

Hope laughed. "I'm a big girl; I can take care of myself."

Her best friend nodded and headed off with the other women.

CHAPTER 2

Hope was left standing with Charles' brother and his friend, and despite what she'd told Grace, nerves made her fidget next to the two men.

Grace's co-star had said their names were Nick and Blaze.

Her bestie was the outgoing one, not her. She wanted to say something but, what?

She couldn't take her eyes off Charles' brother during their introduction.

His blond hair was a mess. It was smooth on the sides and back, but the front and top looked sculpted, yet disheveled.

Hope couldn't see his eyes, but he carried himself with dignity and power.

He wasn't strutting like a peacock but definitely had confidence. She'd hoped to run into him again, and now she stood so close, yet so far.

Why can't I speak to him?

What would I say?

She watched in silence when all the girls went up to be auctioned off. Hope was relieved she'd never have to do that.

When they called Grace on stage, the tattooed guy beside her gestured.

"That's your friend, right?" he asked.

Hope nodded.

"Things are gonna get ugly now. Hold on tight."

Hope cocked her head to one side, then really looked at him. Behind his mask, his eyes were so brown they looked black. The depth of his eyes was what she noticed most.

A girl could get lost in his eyes. With the mask on, she couldn't see his face, but she was curious. Hope understood why her bestie couldn't stop looking at him. He wasn't her type, though.

What is my type?

The auction had started, and her attention was drawn away from Blaze and her internal thoughts.

Blaze called out an offer of five hundred, and again at one thousand. He'd stopped when Nick called his attention.

"What? Why? I thought you wanted Scarlet."

"Didn't you see the way my brother was looking at her? He's totally fallen for his leading lady," Nick said.

"So? Let him have her. You're not really interested, are you?"

"Not that I want to use the girl, but my little brother needs to learn a lesson. He's never been good with sharing. Even as kids, we'd fight all the time over stupid shit, even over whose toothpaste was whose. And it's obvious she has no interest in him. She was staring right at me."

"Wishful thinking, buddy. Not every girl has a thing for you."

"Five thousand dollars!" Nick yelled, instead of replying to Blaze.

Hope's stomach had a seizure.

What does this guy do for a living that he can teach his brother a five thousand dollar lesson?

What she wouldn't give to have that kind of money just lying around.

"Shit, man. Really?" Blaze's voice had an angry edge. He said nothing else as he watched Nick walk away. He turned to Hope, as if she had any clue of what was going on. "Why is it always the blonde that gets the girl?"

"I feel the same way, I mean, it's always the blonde chick that gets the attention."

Blaze laughed. "Yeah, I guess it's true. I've always had a thing for brunettes and redheads, myself. I don't think I have ever dated a blonde. So, do you wanna dance?"

Hope took a step back. He'd caught her off guard. "Um, yeah. That would be nice, thank you."

He offered his hand and led her to the back of the dance floor, where it was less crowded.

She'd wished earlier in the night that she was in the arms of Charles' brother, but Blaze was a blast to hang out with.

He hinted at an interest in her best friend.

It gave her hope; Grace had been alone too long. If she was being honest, Hope wanted Nick.

Could one lead to the other?

She spared a glance at her friend, and her heart sank to her toes.

The chestnut-haired beauty was looking at the tall blond with admiration.

She was totally flirting with the guy! It was so not fair.

I really need to ditch the shyness.

If she'd just said something to Grace before she'd taken off for the auction, her friend would've known Hope was interested in Nick, and she'd be dancing with the right guy.

She smiled at Blaze. He wasn't really her type, but at least he was fun.

A few short songs later, she glanced at her friend and the object of her desire again.

Grace looked different, almost uncomfortable. It seemed like they were moving closer to her and Blaze.

Sure enough, Nick tapped his friend's shoulder. "Dude, switch me."

Hope had never had a dance interrupted in such a manner. Then again, if Nick wanted to dance with her, who was she to argue how he asked?

Her bestie looked relieved to be leaving Nick's arms, but not any happier to be going to another.

Hope tried to lighten the situation. "Be careful, Grace. He's a little crazy," Hope teased.

Her friend was quickly spun away, and they left her with Nick.

"Well, Hello there, Scarlet," the tall blond said, in a sultry voice.

Hope's heart soared and her skin tingled.

So *she* was Scarlet?

Maybe he's interested in me, after all.

"Scarlet?" Hope feigned ignorance.

"Yeah," Nick said. "You know, from *Gone With The Wind*?"

"I know *Gone With The Wind*, but why Scarlet?"

"You have the ringlets and the red dress."

Hope laughed, and her face flushed with a delighted heat.

Scarlet wore a red dress in one scene in the movie, but her dress was fitted to her knees. Rhett had forced her to wear it because she'd been lusting after another man.

Does Nick think I'm a harlot?

"So," she started, quickly changing the direction of her thoughts. "It's none of my business, but why did you feel you needed to teach your brother a lesson?"

"You heard that?"

Is that shame in his eyes?

"I was standing right by you and Blaze. Did you have any clue that your friend is interested in Grace?"

"Blaze? He was just helping me piss off my brother."

"No, Nick, he wasn't."

"Enough about him, tell me about you?"

She stared into his aquamarine eyes. It had to be the mask making his eyes look that bright. Their shade was surreal.

🎼♪♩

WHAT IS it about this woman? I can't let go.

Nick held tight to the full-figured brunette, his eyes locked onto her hazel orbs. There was something about her that drew him in.

What was it?

Hope wasn't his normal flavor of coffee.

He was known for his choice of tall, thin, and blonde. *She* was a fresh drink of water.

Yet perplexing at the same time.

Nick had continued dancing with Grace after their initial song, to further teach his snot-nosed little brother a lesson.

Just because Charles had made a claim didn't mean some-thing, or some*one*, belonged to him. The kid had never gotten that through his head. With a family the size of theirs, it should've been ingrained since birth.

Nick had learned his original assessment was right; Grace had no interest in his brother.

That was a relief.

Charles didn't deserve someone like Grace. Although their relationship was strained, his younger brother had confided all sorts of details about Grace, tuning him in on how deep Charles' feelings ran for the chestnut-haired beauty. He needed to be put in his place.

When he'd admitted he knew a bit too much about Grace, it'd made her uncomfortable and she'd asked him to dance with her friend.

He'd glanced at Hope then, and made a comment about how she looked like someone from a movie.

They'd said in unison, "Scarlet." Then made their way over to the other couple, switching places in a whirl of satin.

One dance led to another.

Nick couldn't let her go.

She'd never acted like she wanted to leave, so he kept her by his side.

For over two hours, they danced and chatted. Not about anything in particular, just common conversation.

Hope was so easy to talk to. She'd never once brought up his job. It was a relief. What he did for a living was usually the first thing women wanted to talk about.

"How about a drink?" Nick whispered in her ear. He loved it when her response was reddened cheeks, rather than words.

Blaze stood alone at the bar.

He made his way to the dark-haired man, keeping his dance partner tucked safely on his arm. "Why you alone?"

"Grace got swept away by her 'father.' So, I thought I'd get a drink. Care to join me?"

Nick ordered himself a Corona and Hope a glass of Moscato. He almost choked on his beer when his brother joined them, satisfaction written on his smug face.

"I see you finally got a clue about Grace," Charles said.

"No, I just found someone I liked more. But fear not, you still have competition, little brother." Nick didn't explain further. He could feel his anger building. This wasn't the time or the place for a blowout. He needed to get away from the situation. But that meant leaving *her.* He took a moment, finishing the last of his beer, weighing his options. He set the empty bottle on the bar and turned to her, ignoring his little brother. "My apologies, Hope. Blaze and I really need to be going. We have another event to go to tomorrow before the show. I hope I'll see you again. Thank you for the wonderful evening." He walked away, leaving Hope alone with Charles.

Charles gave her what she considered a million-watt smile before speaking. "I'm sorry. I don't think I ever got your name." He offered his hand.

"Hope."

He brought her hand to his lips and pressed a tender kiss on her knuckles. "Why is a lady as beautiful as you, spending time with an asshole like my brother?"

"I, um…" She struggled with her reply. Nick had been nothing but a gentleman with her. And Charles was the one being the asshole. "Hey, my feet are killing me. Do you mind if we sit?" Hope glanced at the white granite tile planter box, not far. The wide top would work as a 'seat'.

Charles led her over and sat on her left side, and her skirts filled the space between them.

She smiled. "Thank you. I'd hate to be sitting here all alone, waiting for Grace."

The younger man sighed, and his shoulders caved. "I love my brother, but sometimes he can be such an ass. He kept Grace all to himself, and I never had a chance to dance with her." He sounded so sad.

"Actually, it was me he spent most of the night with," Hope whispered. She tried for a subject change. "So, tell me a little about you. When I was dancing with Blaze, he was saying the musical was popular because of you. Why's that?"

"I've been a pop star since I was about twelve. I've sold over one million albums. A few years ago, I dated some rather popular Hollywood girls, all blondes. That landed me in the spotlight, but not in a good way. I'm done with blondes."

Peacocking much?

His confession should have impressed her, but she found his tone to be cocky.

Hurry, Grace. I don't know how much I can take.

"So why are you doing an off-Broadway play instead of movies or something?"

"I wanted to try something different. I don't like being told what I should do…"

Hope looked to see what had caught his eye when he stopped talking.

Grace was slowly gliding their way.

She stood and hugged her friend. "Are you about ready to go? I'm sure your feet are killing you in those shoes."

"You can't leave. I haven't had a dance yet," Charles protested, jumping up from his seat on the planter box.

Her bestie scoffed. "Charles, we dance together every day. My feet hurt, and I've danced all night."

"Please," he begged.

Hope knew her friend wanted to say no, but her kind heart and friendly nature won over. She'd love to tell Charles off, but she was too shy to speak up.

"Okay, fine. As long as I can take my shoes off first."

He offered his hand so she could bend over and accomplish her task.

"Hope?" Grace asked.

Hope took her pumps. She forced out words that needed to be said, for Charles more than Grace. "Don't worry about me. Just keep it to one song, please?" She stayed where she was, keeping an eye on her friend dancing with her co-star.

The slow circle reminded her of a high school prom number.

There was no rhythm, no direction.

Then they stopped moving.

Grace looked upset. Her cheeks were void of color, and her eyes like sharp daggers.

Had Hope missed something?

Grace walked off the dance floor alone.

She said nothing as she joined her. They walked in silence to the elevator, and the ride was just as quiet.

Hope let her keep to her thoughts.

Grace would open up when she was ready.

They sat on Hope's bed, their dresses unzipped but still pooled around them. She didn't have to share a room like Grace did, so they could have privacy.

Her bestie finally broke the silence, but she didn't gush about the dance with Charles. She begged Hope to spill on the evening.

They both got comfortable in their nests of fabric and dished.

CHAPTER 3

The following evening, Hope found her seat in the theater and glanced around. Her stomach fluttered with disappointment to find the two seats beside her empty.

A theatrical production was always more enjoyable when they filled every seat.

It was just moments before curtain call when there was some sort of disruption at the end of her row.

She laughed when Blaze and Nick tried to work their way through the seated people.

"Is this seat taken?" Blaze asked.

Hope couldn't speak for a moment. "Um, no," was all she could get out. She glanced past the dark-haired man, and her heart skipped when Nick looked right at her, smiling a dazzling smile that lit up his eyes.

Blaze brought her back to reality when he spoke again. "I know it's odd, but would you mind sliding over one seat and sitting in between us? I want to ask you a few questions about Grace, if you don't mind?"

She stood; they did a little dance, switching places. It made her heart soar.

Blaze was showing interest in Grace. Did that mean Nick was into *her*?

This was turning out to be quite an adventure.

Hope waited for curtain-call, and took a deep breath to settle herself.

That was a big mistake.

When she inhaled, she took in the surrounding air, but also a little of Nick. His cologne swirled around her, making her feel kind of drunk.

"Have you seen the show before?" Blaze leaned in, breaking the spell Nick was putting her under.

She was still trying to collect herself from the musky scent of the man to her right. She could only stare at the other man.

"You know, it's okay for you to talk once in a while," Blaze teased.

Before Hope could answer, the curtains opened.

The show was amazing.

She could see the turmoil in Grace, as much in her character, Maddie. She fell in love with the boy-next-door her father had told her she could never have. While events unfolded, Maddie learned there was so much more out in the world.

The character went in search of something dangerous, something magical, only to discover she already had everything she desired in her own front yard.

The ending brought tears to Hope's eyes, and she had to pull a tissue out of her purse to dab at the corners.

Then the show was over, the curtain calls done, and the applause died out.

"You are staying for the cheese and wine tasting, right?" Blaze asked.

Nick interrupted. "Wine?"

"Dude, you're an idiot. Didn't you see the sign when we came in? They're hosting a cheese and wine party to raise money for the company. Damn, pay attention."

Hope touched his shoulder. "Of course, I'm going. Grace is my best friend and I'm here to support her."

"Then may I offer you my arm and escort you?"

"I would be de—" She didn't get to finish the sentence because Nick appeared on her other side and offered his arm without asking.

Blaze made a sound that sounded like a muffled laugh and touched her arm, to bring her attention back to him. "I really want you to tell me a little bit about her. The sooner the better," he whispered right above her ear.

Hope didn't get to divulge any information because Grace and Charles headed toward them.

She broke contact with the two men and enfolded her best friend into a tight embrace. "What a fabulous show, Gracie, I think this was the best one yet."

"Thank you. I was really into character."

Nick kissed her friend's knuckles. "Impressive, Grace. I was almost brought to tears at the end. It was a very emotional scene. Even my brother poured everything into it."

Envy hit her gut. She never wanted to be in the spotlight, but to have him kiss her hand like that… Hope wanted to swoon.

🎼

NICK TURNED TO HOPE. He was burning for a moment alone with her. "Would you like to join me for a drink?"

"Um, yes, that would be lovely."

He offered her his arm, which fit so perfectly in the crook of his.

Why does it feel like this?

"What can I get for you?" the bartender asked Hope.

"I'll take a Moscato if you have it," she said in a quiet voice.

"And for you, sir?"

"Your best red wine, the drier the better."

"Yes, sir."

He didn't normally have more than one drink a week; it was part of his new healthier lifestyle, but he needed something to take off the edge.

I shouldn't need liquid courage. I'm Nick fucking Ford! Women fall at my feet!

Drinks in hand, they worked their way back to their friends, just in time to see Blaze's face red from laughing.

Nick put his hand on his friend's shoulder. "What's so funny?"

His buddy appeared to be having a hard time catching his breath; his face was blotchy, and he was panting through his chuckles. "Dude, she thinks we're porn stars!"

He frowned and scratched his head. They'd been accused of being many things, but porn stars hadn't been one that'd ever hit the list before.

"No really, Blaze. What do you *do* for a living then?" Grace asked.

"I'm in the entertainment industry. I'm a stage performer." There was a brief pause. "I'm sure you already know who I am. So let's quit playing games," his friend said. He had a dark eyebrow arched.

Nick tried not to laugh at the hidden pun.

She really doesn't know who we are?

Everyone knew who they were. Nick let out a sigh. They couldn't go anywhere without being mobbed. This was so surreal.

"I'm sorry, Blaze. I don't know who you are, other than a friend of Charles's brother. So yes, let's quit playing games."

They could have cut the tension in their little circle with a knife.

Since he'd defused many intense situations as a big brother, Nick stepped up to the plate. "I'm surprised my brother hasn't told you all about us. You know he has a musical background, correct?"

"Yes," Grace snapped. "I knew one of his songs when it first came out. I think it was called *Beat Back?*"

"Yeah, that's right. But did you know he had an older brother in a pop band?"

He glanced at Hope just as the pink rose in her cheeks. "So you have heard of us, then? *Razor's Edge…*"

Grace spoke, bringing his eyes back to her. "I don't keep up with the music scene. I mean, there are a few songs I love, I'll catch on the radio once in a while or on a playlist, but I don't follow bands."

Hope leaned into her friend. "You know that song you like, *Unfinished?* I think that's them." Her voice was a stage-whisper, and Nick wanted to smile.

"Are you sure?"

Yes, the song was one of theirs.

He felt a twinge of anticipation in his stomach. At least Hope knew who they were. And she wasn't acting like the typical fan, freaking out like they do.

Hope pulled her phone out and typed something. She turned it around, showing them.

The results showed the artist was *Razor's Edge*.

"Okay, all that proves is the name of the band was right. That doesn't mean *they're* a part," Grace pointed out.

He shot Blaze a look, and a grin crept across his friend's face. He knew exactly what Nick was thinking.

They nodded at each other, took a step closer and sang in perfect pitch and harmony.

"PRETENDING YOU WERE NEVER HERE, Stuck in a world of dreams,
　Wishing I could heal my heart, All I do is scream,
　Without you I am, Unfinished."

. . .

WHEN THEY FINISHED, Nick glanced at Hope, hoping for the recognition that usually came with the knowledge of who he was.

"That's cool. So what're you drinking tonight?" Grace asked Hope.

His attention was yanked away from the object of his desire when her friend spoke. He blinked, and his words vanished.

Blaze scoffed. "'*That's cool*'? We tell you we are part of the number one pop band in the world and all you can say is '*that's cool*'?"

"Not to insult you or anything, Blaze, but yeah, *that's cool*. It doesn't change anything. You're still the nice dark-eyed guy I danced with last night. Would you prefer I fawn all over you?"

"Hey, Grace, can I talk to you for a sec?" Some guy from the play pulled the actress away from their circle.

Nick stood in stunned silence that obviously mirrored his friend's. He subtly watched Hope as all this went down, trying to gauge her reaction, too.

She wasn't as aloof as her friend was, but she also wasn't fawning like he'd expected; like he was used to.

"I promise, she's normally not this snarky," Hope told Blaze. "She's just been a little stressed. If you give her another chance..."

Blaze smiled, and Nick narrowed his eyes a little.

What was his friend up to?

"Actually, I find it quite refreshing. Because of my bad-boy appearance and attitude, people have a tendency to avoid confrontation with me. She's a little spitfire. She kind of reminds me of my Nana." His buddy cocked his head to the side. "There's one thing I don't get."

"What's that?" Hope asked.

"Not to sound cocky, but how can she not know who I am? Everyone knows *Razor's Edge*. Don't they?"

Nick snorted. His friend wasn't wrong.

She let out a deep breath. "Well, look at it this way. I love the song *Moves Like Jagger* and I know it's by *Maroon 5*. But I couldn't tell you any other songs they have, let alone the names or faces of the band members. She may not know any other songs by your group. Don't take it personally."

Blaze's face changed. Softened.

That wasn't easy for the bad-boy to do. People often feared Blaze's backlash, but not this woman. Grace really was different. Maybe she'd be the right one for his buddy.

What about *him*?

Nick stepped closer, slipping his arm around Hope's shoulder.

She molded into the groove of his body.

He'd had plenty of women tucked right where the petite brunette was nestled, but they never *felt* like this.

Perfect.

He put his cheek on the top of her head and let out a little sigh. "It just amazes me how perfectly you fit here."

Shit, did I say that out loud?

Panic made him fidget.

Why had he said that? It was a weird-comforting feeling when he touched her, like they'd known each other for years instead of hours.

Hope's body tensed at his words.

Don't fuck this up, boy. For Blaze's sake, yeah. My buddy needs to hook up with Grace.

"Don't worry, little one. I'd like to get to know every little thing about you." He moved to look down at her.

His gaze was so intense, she broke their eye contact and glanced over at Blaze.

"You know, it'd be okay if you want to talk to her," she said.

It hit Nick hard that she was avoiding him now, even though she was still under his arm.

"That's okay. I'm enjoying the view. Besides, she's doing her thing. I can tell she's good at working the crowd. What kind of guys does she like? What kind of guys has she dated?"

Hope's cheeks flush red from the question. "I, um… I have no clue if Grace has dated anyone in the past three years."

"Really?" Blaze asked.

"I live too far away," she whispered, before turning to those gorgeous eyes back on him. "Uh, Nick," she began. "Tell me a little about yourself."

"That could take all night," Blaze teased.

"All right, just the basics then." His lady smiled, and the pink on her cheeks was so charming.

Nick flashed his best smile, ignoring his buddy. "Well, I'm the oldest of six kids, Charles and Angel are the youngest. We're the only boys, too, so most of the time it was just him and me. I joined *Razor's Edge* when I was twelve, and the rest is history."

She slipped out of his arms to set her empty wine glass on the bar.

He felt empty without her there.

Nick reached for her, bringing her back into his embrace again. He couldn't help himself. He remembered what she'd said about Maroon 5. Maybe she didn't know their history.

Good, then she doesn't know about my past.

It would be the first time in his life he'd get a clean slate.

He wouldn't… no, couldn't, lose his chance with this one.

But what about her?

Did she have secrets that could destroy him?

"Don't worry about me, it's you I want to get to know."

"Oh, there's not much to me. I'm just… nobody."

"Trust me, you *are* somebody. I want to know more."

Hope took a deep breath. "I'm the youngest. I have two older brothers, and a sister. I'm not close to them. We have a bit of an age difference. My life is rather boring. I'm an insurance adjuster. Oh, and my companions… I have three dogs…"

Nick chuckled. "Well, the dogs might be an issue; I have a mild allergy."

"An issue?" Hope asked. A frown marred her pretty face, and she sounded confused.

"Yeah, when we 'get to know each other better'. I don't want to be sneezing all over you."

"I, um… I need to use the ladies' room." She excused herself and practically ran from him.

CHAPTER 4

Hope stared at herself in the mirror. Her cheeks were flushed red.

What the hell's going on here?

She couldn't believe things were happening the way they were.

Did a conversation mean 'something happened?'

Nick had scared her.

Why did he think he'd ever spend time with her dogs?

He'd certainly wanted nothing more than a one-night-stand, wouldn't he?

Was she even interested in something like that? It wasn't something she'd ever entertained before, but could Hope say no to someone as good looking as Nick?

It wasn't every day a bonafide popstar showed interest in her.

He was famous.

She ran her hands under the water, reveling in the cold. She put her hands up to her face, and the shock to her hot skin was exactly what she needed. Hope sighed, shut off the water and headed out of the bathroom.

"Thank you for letting me tell Ms. Grace the news about her

permanent position in the company. I think she's going to be a great fit in L.A., don't you think?"

She overheard an older gentleman say. There was a tall blond man talking to him.

"Indeed, Grace is perfect to join our theater. Actor and promoter? I couldn't ask for a better pers…"

Hope didn't hear the rest of the conversation, since they walked just out of earshot, but the news of her best friend's future overjoyed her. She smiled when she rejoined the two gorgeous men.

She and Grace could do worse.

Nick slipped his hand to glide round her waist the moment she was within reaching distance.

Hope was still in disbelief, and didn't move. However, there wasn't an opportunity to comment, because Blaze stepped away and Grace rejoined them.

"The party's winding down. I've got to get out of costume. I'll be quick, but it usually takes me about forty-five minutes. Do you want to meet back at the hotel or hang out here?" Her friend's voice was quiet, mostly likely for Hope's ears only.

Their present company overheard.

"Actually," Nick interrupted. "There's a bar right across the street. Blaze and I would be more than glad to keep Hope company."

Grace chewed at her bottom lip, with obvious nerves, looking around the room.

Hope followed her friend's eyes when they rested on the dark-haired man standing at the bar.

"I should apologize to Blaze. I was rude. But I'm not sure I have it in me to have another late night, though," Grace said.

"Just come for a little while," she said. She needed to spend more time with Nick. Needed to get to the bottom of things. "I'll make sure you leave early enough."

Grace nodded and hugged her before heading backstage.

Blaze returned to them, and Nick quickly explained their plans for the night.

"Hell, yeah. I'm totally up for keeping this one company," he said, winking at Hope.

Her face burned all over, and her heart sped up.

Once again, both men slipped an arm through her own, escorting her across the street to the bar.

HOPE GLANCED AROUND THE ESTABLISHMENT. Straight back was a long bar, hundreds of liquor bottles lined up behind the bartender.

Tables and chairs were scattered throughout, with various people standing around. There was a large dance floor to the right, and to the left were four pool tables.

Nick took her hand, the heat from his skin radiating through her body, leaving her slightly stunned.

His interest in her was…surreal.

Exciting, and scary.

It couldn't be real?

Without a word, he led her to the bar. He didn't let go of her when he leaned against it, and gave the man behind the counter his order, a Corona for both him and Blaze.

"What are you having?" he inquired.

Hope laughed when they both called out to the bartender for a *Sex on the Beach*.

He flashed a devilish smile; the sparkle coming back into his intense blue eyes.

"Yes, please," she whispered. Hope's cheeks flushed with heat all over, so she looked down at her hands, avoiding his hot gaze.

How did I get here?

An hour ago, they'd been enjoying cheese and wine, and his arm had snaked around her.

When Nick had expressed that he wanted to get to know her, she couldn't have been more stunned.

Why?

Hope had always suffered from mild depression, which was funny, considering her name.

She'd had her heart broken so viciously a few years ago, and would never trust a man again. She was very suspicious of Nick and his actions.

Nick gently ran the tips of his fingers over the back of her right hand. "What did you do to me, little one?"

Hope shifted a little closer to make sure she heard him right. "Excuse me?"

What was he talking about?

"You make me feel like I'm any other guy. I don't think I've ever felt this way before. It's a little weird."

Hope blinked.

What could she say?

He was just like any guy.

"I don't know what I did. I mean, I just met you and all, but..." She stumbled for words.

The bartender rescued her, handing them their drinks.

"*This* is what I am talking about. You just found out I'm part of the most popular pop band in the world, and you still act like this. Were you just about any other girl..." He shook his head, but didn't finish.

Hope had an idea.

Nick probably had women rubbing up against him all the time, trying to get a little attention.

She wasn't like that. She was more than happy to stay out of the light.

To have a guy paying attention to her was a little scary.

Especially a guy like him.

He gave her hand a gentle tug, and headed straight for the pool tables. "Wanna play?"

"Pool?" she asked.

"Well, that's all we can play right now, so, yeah. Pool." He winked.

Hope had to look away.

What the heck was happening?

She looked at Blaze, and the small smile on his lips traveled to fill his dark eyes with light.

Things were about to get frisky for her best friend.

Was the same happening for her?

The rustling of acrylic balls behind her caught her attention. Nick was stocking the balls into a wooden triangle.

What a view.

His dark jeans showed off his assets really nicely. When he bent over to add another ball to the setup, a white belt peeked out from under the light blue shirt he wore.

He was…delicious.

She needed to relax. A guy that looked like him had never been into Hope.

She could have a little fun with the popstar. It wasn't like it meant forever.

Blaze stood to her right side. He stayed silent while Nick sank another ball. Then he coughed, as if trying to get the courage to ask Hope something. He finally spoke. "Do you think she'll get here soon?"

She tried not to laugh.

That's what he wanted to ask me?

She'd been praying for something better, something to help her understand Nick.

His interest in her friend was there, but he hadn't really asked anything juicy yet.

Hope put her hand on his shoulder, and they made eye contact. "She's coming. Don't worry."

.   .   .

"READY?" Nick asked, making direct eye contact.

She was learning fast that it was what he was prone to and she needed to stop letting it freak her out. Hope cleared her throat. "I think I'll let you two play a round first." She gently shook her drink, letting the ice tink against the glass.

"Only this once. You'll play the winner of this one."

Nick went first, sending the balls in all directions, sinking a striped ball. He missed on the next shot. He moved over to stand by her left side while Blaze took his turn.

Hope sat on a high bar stool, and put the heels of her shoes behind the only rung on the front of the chair, for a bit of stability in an otherwise unsure situation.

Nick leaned ever so slightly against her legs, and she was bold, testing her and his limits.

"GOOD CHOICE! Since you got one in, you get to go again. Shall I help you?"

Hope could only nod. Her heart tripped again. She might not really need the help, but she wanted his body on hers. The thrill of it shot down her spine.

Nick positioned himself behind her, exactly the same as he'd done before. Only this time, he pressed a little closer to her. "Do you see the line?"

"I think so."

"Pull back and release."

She was just about to do so, when out of the corner of her eye, Grace stepped into view. Embarrassment overtook the delicious temptation. Hope popped up from the risqué position.

Blaze pushed off the wall and closed the distance between them and Grace. He pulled her friend into his arms.

"Um, hi Blaze?" Grace sputtered.

They both needed a moment to get away from all the testosterone around them.

"Come to the bar with me and get a drink?" Hope moved away from Nick.

Grace nodded.

When they got to the bar, Hope leaned into the counter. She had a secret. "You need to have a drink," she told her best friend.

"Thank you, but I'll wait until tomorrow."

"No, Grace, you won't. You need to celebrate tonight."

"Not until tomorrow. I give certain things up during a production."

She'd had enough. She'd overheard a little about what lay ahead for her dearest friend, not only with the theater, but the potential with Blaze.

The girl needed to get a clue.

"You need to be honest with yourself. I know you forgo liquor for your plays, but you gave up having relationships *permanently*. You really need to move on."

Her friend's back went ramrod-stiff and she clenched her fists tight. Grace blew out the breath she held and started to walk away.

Hope grabbed her arm, spinning her friend back to face her. "I don't mean the loss of your parents, damn it! I meant *him*… You can't let one bad night with some asshole ruin the rest of your life. He wins if you never let yourself live! I think you have a very hot man just feet away, ready to bend over backward for you. Or bend you over backward. Either way, it's time."

The wheels turning in Grace's head were visible on her face.

Maybe Hope had hit a nerve after all.

"I overheard something tonight, on my way to the ladies' room, about you permanently joining the company?"

Grace stared, but didn't speak.

"So it's true? That's amazing and definitely something to celebrate! It's only one drink." Not waiting for a reply, Hope pulled her cellphone out of her back pocket and looked at the screen. Then she laughed.

"What's so funny?"

"I have this awesome app called *Mixology*. It tells you how to make different drinks. We have to have this one." She flashed the picture on the screen.

Her friend laughed with her and agreed.

With their drinks in hand, they headed back to the pool table, and back to Nick and Blaze.

She reached for his soft, tousled hair. Her fingers slid along his scalp, finding pure joy in the innocent, yet seductive way she was touching him.

The soft moan that escaped his lips said he enjoyed it as much as she did.

Blaze missed on his turn, and Nick had to step away to play. He sank a solid yellow ball.

The game went on just a little longer.

Blaze won, but offered to let Nick play in his stead.

Her would-be beau set up the ball for another round. "Pick a stick," he called.

HOPE STOOD before the display of pool cues, unsure which to choose. It'd been years since she played pool. She wasn't very good.

"That one looks perfect," Nick whispered in her ear.

Hope hadn't heard him move closer to her. Gooseflesh rippled over her skin when the heat of his breath washed over her. She stepped forward, away from him, and grabbed the first cue in front of her. She didn't answer him.

"You can break, and choose stripes or solids."

She stepped up to the table and let out a puff of breath. She tried to eye up the ball but made the mistake of glancing up.

Nick stood across from her, his blue gaze hungry.

One glance down told her he could see right down her pink scoop neck top. Her face seared.

Hope should be pleased, not embarrassed, that he liked what he could see, right?

She chided herself to relax.

Just play pool.

She tried to stand up a little more, at least get her shoulders higher, but that put her at a major disadvantage to getting a line of sight on the ball.

Hope pulled her right arm back, holding the cue. Her left hand grazed the green fabric of the pool table, and her right hand thrust the cue stick forward.

The tip hit hard on the right of the white ball, sending it spinning awkwardly into the nicely arranged balls.

Not one sank into a pocket.

In fact, they barely moved.

Across from her, Blaze chuckled.

Embarrassment kissed her cheeks again, and she looked away.

"Bro, I think she could use a little help. I'll set them again. Go show her how to do it," Blaze said.

Nick ran his fingertips across the lip of the table, caressing the wood as he made his way closer to her.

Hope's heart pumped hard, thundered her ears with the sound of blood rushing through her body. She wanted to reach up to her neck to make sure the pulsing wasn't visible.

"May I?" he drawled. Nick didn't wait for a response. He slipped a hand across her lower back, letting her know he was behind her. He moved so close, their bodies pressed together. He gave her a gentle push, and she leaned forward.

Their height difference made it possible for him to lean over her body and still line up the ball perfectly.

His left hand went to hers, showing her a better way to hold for aiming. His right hand slid down the length of her arm, trialing heat as he went.

His breath tickled her ear as he spoke to her in hushed tones. "Imagine there's a line from the end of the stick to the middle of the ball. Pull back, but not too far. Just enough to give it the force it needs to propel forward. Yeah, just…like…this."

Together they shot the white cue ball, breaking the others to scatter across the table.

Two solids crashed into the side pockets.

Hope laughed, full of joy as Nick stood back up. She'd sunk two balls. One solid, one striped. She looked over her shoulder at him, a little confused.

"You get to choose. What do you want to be?"

"Solids!" she called.

CHAPTER 5

"Ready to finish this?" Nick asked as Hope set the drink on the small table next to Blaze.

"I'm really not good at this. Maybe you two should just take over." She glanced at the dark-haired man. Tried not to laugh, because the lusty look in those dark eyes had locked on her best friend.

"You got this, babe." Nick brought her attention back to him. "I'll help you line up again if you need it."

As much as Hope wouldn't mind having him pressed against her body again, her hormones couldn't take it.

Or her heart.

Focus on the game, girl. Not him.

She tried her best, keeping her eyes strictly on the green felt in front of her.

Nick took pity on her, yet he still won the game.

She was more than happy to pass her cue stick on to someone else.

He racked the balls to prepare for another game, and Blaze disappeared to the bar.

"Hey, Gracie," Nick said. "You're up next."

"Um, okay. So, who am I playing?"

"Well, I beat Hope, so I guess you're playing me."

Hope flashed a devilish grin. Once again, she carried a secret.

"I'm warning you, Nick. I suck," Grace admitted. Her cheeks were flushed red from the alcohol.

It gave Hope, well… some *hope* for her best friend's future. Her bestie needed to let loose and find some joy in life outside of the theater.

Blaze came back to the pool table with a bright blue drink in his hand and offered it to Grace.

"What's this?" she asked.

"It's a *BJ in the Morning.*" He winked.

Hope was envious again.

Blaze clearly had feelings for Grace. The look in his eyes said it was more than a one-night stand.

She glanced at Nick.

What are his intentions?

"Grace, you have to break to determine if you're solids or stripes," Nick said, bringing Hope back to the game at hand.

Her bestie purposely messed up when scattering the balls. Grace obviously wanted the guys to think she didn't know how to play pool very well.

"I can help you, if you'd like," Blaze offered.

Hope tried not to laugh when, a moment later, Grace was in the same position she'd been in with Nick just a short time before.

Little did they know Grace was an expert. Her father had taught her from a young age how to play.

On more than one occasion, they'd come home from the bar with more money than they'd started with because men would bet they could beat her.

When it was her friend's turn, and she was playing a different kind of game with Blaze, Nick came to stand by Hope again.

The liquid courage helped. She put her hands on his shoulders and guided him, so he stood in between her knees. Her chin fit perfectly on his shoulder.

He reached behind to grab at her hands. He put them on his chest, letting her know he wanted more, too. Every time it was Grace's turn, Nick returned to Hope and her touch.

It was fun to watch her would-be man get cocky, like he had the win in the bag.

Then Grace played her way and soon, Nick was getting his ass kicked.

He sighed in defeat. He'd lost this round, but it was looking like Blaze was going to win overall. "Hey! I thought you said you suck."

Grace laughed, and the alcohol spoke for her. She glanced at Blaze. "I do suck. I suck good."

His face flushed crimson.

Hope burst out laughing, proud of her friend for relaxing, even if it was a little much.

There were a couple guys waiting for them to finish their round so they could have a turn at the table, so Nick suggested they hit the dance floor.

"Oh, I don't know…" Hope said.

"I won't take no for an answer. I *need* your body."

She snapped her head up, and collided with the heat in his eyes.

Nick continued to move toward the floor, her hand buried in his.

On the dance floor, everything and everyone disappeared.

Nick pulled her against his chest. Although they had quite a height difference, they fit together like two puzzle pieces.

Hope laced her fingers through his hair, and in return, he ran his fingertips along the underside of her arms, which was now exposed.

She'd never really been ticklish, but it was sending sparks throughout her body.

His hand continued down her body to find the edge of her belt, and his thumb caught in the edge, holding her even closer to him.

She could feel the heat of his body, and the way he was reacting to her pressed against him.

The evidence was exciting and terrifying.

Hope had never had a one-night stand.

Could she say yes?

Could she say no?

What did she *want*?

It brought her out of her Nick bubble when she spotted Grace leaving with Blaze. In a hurry.

She hoped things would go well.

"Elvis has left the building," she whispered.

Nick nuzzled her neck, "Elvis?"

"Yeah," she said breathlessly, the heat of his breath getting the best of her. "Her name, Grace Lynn, sounds like Graceland... so, Elvis."

Had her words made any sense? She felt garbled and faraway. Out of her own skin.

Nick laughed. "I'll have to tell Blaze about that one."

The song had ended, and a new mix was beginning.

His body tensed suddenly.

Did I do something wrong?

Hope stepped away and faced him, her stomach clenched.

Nick leaned in close to her ear. "We may have to leave...soon."

"What's wrong?" She had a slight flutter of hope because he'd said 'we'.

"Um," he bit his lower lip. "This is me."

"What's you?" she asked, frowning.

"This song. It's me singing. It's called, *Aflame*."

"Then let's dance," Hope said. She continued to face him, and they seduced each other on the dance floor.

Nick visibly relaxed, and he sang along.

He was some huge popstar, boybander. *Razor's Edge.*

Did it change how she felt about him?

No. Not at all.

Their dancing was more like making love with their clothes still on.

Hope was so hot by the time the song was over, she had to take a break. "Do you mind if we step outside and get some air?"

He didn't answer; Nick just took her hand and led her out.

She'd expected him to go to the patio. The door leading out was just before the pool tables, but he slipped them out the front door. "Let's get outta here."

♪

IT WAS ALREADY after one a.m., and Hope found herself back in her room, with Nick trailing right behind.

There'd been no intention of bringing him up, yet there they were.

"I, um…"

What should she say?

"Well, look at it this way; the room I share with Blaze is most likely occupied."

"If you are such a big star, couldn't you afford your own room?" she teased.

"There was only one room left at our favorite hotel, so we shared. That way we could just go to the events without having to worry about meeting up and getting mobbed alone. It's always better to get recognized in a small group rather than when solo."

That made sense.

Now, Hope was in a situation she hadn't planned for.

Her hands shook when she put the keycard against the locking pad. She pushed the door open and flipped on the light.

She remembered her brief chastising of herself from earlier in the day; she'd forgotten to put the "Privacy" card on the door.

They'd serviced the room, including making the bed, and placed fresh towels in the bathroom.

Nick reached around her, holding the door so she could enter.

The heavy panel slammed back with a finalizing click.

He walked around the room and stuck his head in the bathroom. "Wow, that tub looks comfortable."

Although there were no jets in it, Hope had to admit the oversized oval-shaped tub looked inviting. She'd always preferred baths to showers. "Would you like a bath?"

He nodded.

She started the water before stepping out of the room. Nerves skittered below the surface of her skin, despite the alcohol. Hope kicked off her heels right away, hoping it would ease her tension.

His breath on her neck caught her off guard. She hadn't heard him step up behind her.

"Can I unzip that for you?" Nick asked, his voice a low, sexy rumble.

"I'm joining you?"

"Of, course," he whispered into her ear while pushing her hair over her left shoulder, exposing her bare neck and shoulder. He unhooked the top clasp and unzipped her blouse.

She covered her breasts when her top fell to the floor. She wasn't wearing a bra.

His hands slid around her, caressing her soft flesh.

She tilted her head back, as her body pressed against him, as if of its own accord.

He kissed her shoulder, then her neck.

Her heart raced. She whirled to face him.

This was it.

No going back.

If it was going to be a one-night stand, she'd enjoy every minute.

Mettle she'd never had before urged her on.

Hope urged his T-shirt up over his head.

She gasped when his hands came down to find her waist, then slid to the front to unbutton her jeans before he peeled them down her legs.

She held back a groan of pleasure as Nick kissed the tops of her thighs while he moved the fabric, lower and lower. She stepped out of her pants.

He held her close, their tongues danced as she undid his pants, freeing his erection.

She slid her hands over his tight butt and down his legs, urging him out of his pants. Hope stood and turned off the water. She quickly got out of her thong, and held a hand out to him, inviting him to join her.

Her bravery was puzzling, but she was clinging to it, letting it lead her.

This wasn't her. She wasn't a sexpot, but he made her feel like she was.

Hope ran her fingertips up his muscular chest, around his neck, into his hair.

He slid his hands over her butt, lifting her off the ground.

Her legs instinctively wrapped around him as she kissed him.

Nick stepped into the tub, and she wasn't worried he would drop her.

The water was warm as they sank in deep. Hope readjusted her legs so her knees folded beneath her. She leaned in, kissing him again, and placing her hands on the tub wall behind him.

His touch traced her thighs to her hips. He groaned when she ground against him.

Her lips moved to his neck. The slow undulation of her hips felt good to her, even though she was teasing him. Tingles shot down Hope's spine, and she told herself to stay relaxed, go with the flow. She'd been doing so well.

Nick's hands roamed her back when she moved her mouth to his ear.

She sucked first on his earlobe, then ran her tongue around the outside groove.

His body hardened even more beneath, making her ache to have him inside her, ached for him to take control.

Hope slid her fingers between. She gently adjusted him to the right position.

Passion consumed her as she thrust herself down on him.

His hands tightened on her waist as she moved.

She rose to her knees, moving in a delicious rhythm over him. Her body was built for this, her hips rocking back and forth as she slid up and down him.

She had full control as her orgasm built. Hope moved faster.

Nick tried to help, lifting himself to her as she came down harder and faster.

She cried out, throwing her head back as she came. She didn't stop, but leaned into him, rubbing her breasts against his chest.

Hope rode Nick until his body exploded inside her.

He clutched her tight as his body shook with ferocity.

She relaxed against his chest.

Nick caressed up and down her back. "Wow, I've never done it in water." He laughed softly.

"I'm glad I got to be your first," Hope whispered, her head still on his chest.

Hope stood in the bathroom, the door closed while she brushed her teeth. Her head was all over the place.

If someone had asked her a week before what she thought her future held, *this* would not have been it.

Not that she wasn't happy; she was beyond blissful.

It'd happened so quickly.

Hope had finally reconnected with her old friend. It was a relationship they'd both cherished but had neglected.

She had so much to look forward to with Grace's friendship. She'd never again let them drift as far apart as they had become.

Now... she had something new and unbelievably exciting happening.

In the other room, a few feet away, fast asleep, was a possible future.

With Nick's lifestyle, Hope would be lucky to be just a one-night stand.

That wasn't what she wanted.

To have a man like him desire her was mind blowing. Not to mention, Nick had instigated.

He'd been so kind, so genuine while Grace was busy with her show.

Nick had had a friend to spend time with, so he wasn't showing interest in Hope out of boredom. He'd been there to see his brother perform, not to find some girl to hook up with.

Could they really be more?

CHAPTER 6

Hope stretched all her muscles, loving the delicious soreness.

Nick had taken his time with her, making sure her needs were seen to first.

She'd never had a guy do that before.

The man beside her, still asleep, rolled over to face her, looking far too innocent for the truth. Strands of his dark blonde hair had fallen forward on his cheek, which was pink from heated sleep.

His dark lashes would make any woman jealous. His breathing was even and slow.

As soon as she moved to climb out of bed, Nick seemed wide awake.

"Good morning, sunshine," he said, his voice gravelly.

Hope's cheeks flushed with heat. "Morning."

"Where're you going?"

"Um, just the bathroom."

"Wanna leave your clothes in there while you're at it?"

Her stomach flipped.

He wants to see me naked? In the daylight?

A little rumble escaped his throat; soft laughter.

At first, it made her heart sink, filling her with dread.

Had she misread what he'd said?

"Damn, woman. I'd love to keep you naked all day, but I've got to get going."

His words made her heart skip again, but they took all doubts from her.

"I've got an important meeting this afternoon with the band, and I need to get Blaze's ass moving. God knows that guy's lost without guidance. But I'll see you tonight. Charles left us tickets for the last show. And an invitation to the after-party."

The knots in her belly changed, but didn't dissipate. They went from fear of him not wanting her, to nervousness that he *did*.

Why would he want someone like me? I'm no supermodel. Not even close.

She slipped into the bathroom and turned on the hot water.

"NICK, FOCUS!"

Nick met his bandmate's gaze. The deep green of Scott's eyes burned into him.

The oldest member of the group gave him a harsh look, like the big brother he was. "Where were you just now, kid? We really need you to pay attention."

He shook his head to clear his thoughts. A dark-haired, curvy girl was invading his thoughts. He couldn't figure out why.

She wasn't his type, not by far. No matter, he was drawn to her.

It was unmistakable, the way they fit together, in so many ways.

Hope was everything Nick never knew he wanted. He just wanted to get back to her.

"So, we'll start the tour in Chicago in six weeks. That doesn't leave a lot of time for rehearsals," their manager explained. "*Next Step* will be working on their choreography in New York. Eddie's still working full time there on some movie."

"Wait...what? *Next Step?*"

Nick had been lost in thought, but *that* lost?

"Seriously, dude, we've been talking about this joint tour for two years," Blaze said.

"I know, but with Scott back after taking a few years off, I figured we'd put the joint tour on hold. I thought we were staying in L.A. and cutting a new album first." Bile built in his throat. He loved touring. But not now. Not when he needed to be in L.A., where *she* was.

Damn! Why are you getting to me like this?

"Have you been paying attention at all today? That was the first thing we discussed. Nick, are you hungover?" Dwaine, another of his bandmates, asked.

"No," he whispered.

He tried to focus the rest of the meeting. Nick couldn't stop thinking about her lush curves, her soft chocolate hair, the smell of their sex.

She intrigued him. He'd never had a woman so wrapped in his head before.

It was driving him crazy.

He only had four weeks to figure her out.

Would it take that long?

They started in eight days, rehearsing for four weeks at a small studio in Burbank, just outside of L.A., before heading to Chicago.

There, they'd join with the five members of *Next Step*, another very famous pop group.

Next Step had been around about ten years before *Razor's Edge*. They'd taken a break when bubblegum music had been pushed aside to bring in grunge.

When pop started rising the charts again, they'd come out of retirement. Their fifth tour since returning was a joint tour with *Razor's Edge.*

The men from both groups had become good friends over the years, and everyone had been looking forward to the tour.

God only knows what can happen between now and then.

NICK'S HEART slammed against his ribs when the vision of Hope came into sight. He and Blaze had gotten to the theater early this time; they both were anxious to see the show.

Yeah, right.

Neither one expressed their actual reason for wanting to make the evening go faster, but it wasn't a shocker.

She floated toward them like a butterfly.

The sheer blue fabric that flowed around her legs made his cock come alive. He had to bite the inside of his cheek to bring himself back to earth.

The dark blue of her underdress was fitted around her ample bust, showing every beautiful curve on the way down, to end just above her knees.

Over the entire thing was a light blue, sheer, overdress. It was tied with little strings, just below her bust, and flowed to the ground. When she walked, it billowed out and caressed her legs when she stopped.

He wanted to see it on the floor, next to his bed.

Stop it. Now is not *the time!*

Nick offered her his arm without saying a word.

This time, Blaze didn't put her in the middle of them.

He missed most of the show. At least the one on stage.

His eyes remained on Hope, watching the show through her eyes.

Her face was so expressive. Her eyes lit up when something

funny happened. She cried when the characters cried. She contorted her face in confusion toward the end of the show.

The ending scene.

That was when Nick finally looked on stage. It took him a moment to realize why.

This performance was nothing like the night before. There was serious tension between his brother and Grace.

This was their issue, not their characters.

Good thing this is the last night.

Nick could tell his brother wasn't in a good place at that moment, but he didn't want to concentrate on Charles.

"Are you coming to the after-party?" Hope asked when the show was over.

They were her first words since they'd parted that morning.

He tried to listen for anything hidden in her tone, but it was simply a question. He smiled and watched her cheeks flush pink like he knew they would.

Nick had made her cheeks stay that color most of the night before. It didn't take much. A smile, a soft touch. Simple. That meant a lot to him.

"I hope you don't mind if I do."

Her reply was a shake of her head, and a deepening color in her cheeks.

"May I escort you?"

Again, she nodded and Nick offered his arm.

Nick, Hope, and Blaze sat at a table in the hotel's ballroom. The same place the masquerade had been two nights before.

It looks so different now. Gone were the strobe lights and decorations. The only thing the same was the dance floor and the tables and chairs.

They all had a drink in hand, but no one seemed to be drinking.

Except for his brother, who Nick had been watching closely as he hung out at the bar. He resented the attention he'd had to leave on his brother, but Charles didn't seem to be going anywhere. Maybe deeper into his cups.

"So, where in L.A. do you live? I wonder if we've ever crossed paths somewhere, like the grocery store," he said to Hope.

She looked down at her drink, swishing the melting ice around. "I don't live in L.A. Actually, it's my first time here."

Surprise washed over him. He hadn't pressed her to reveal where she was from, his mind whirled at a thousand different places he'd love to show her. Nick started listing off places, watching her face to see if there was a spark to any of them. "There's the Hollywood sign, but that's a walk, or the Griffith Observatory, or maybe Sunset Boulevard, Rodeo Drive…"

"Um, yeah? That all sounds great. And I'd love to but, I need to spend as much time as I can with Grace. I never get to see her."

"Let's bring her along. And Blaze." He glanced at his friend. "What do you think?"

Blaze didn't reply.

"Dude, hello?" Nick waved his hand in front of his buddy's face.

"Yeah, I know what you mean," Blaze said, but he was still looking at the entryway.

"You know what I mean about what? I asked you if you wanted to join Hope and me tomorrow to check out some sights in L.A."

Grace stepped up to them.

Hope left her high bar chair to stand to hug her. She whispered something in Grace's ear, but Nick didn't catch what. Whatever it was made Grace's cheeks bright red. She didn't answer, but joined them at their table.

Grace and Blaze quietly conversed, so he turned back to Hope and his pursuit of events for the next day.

"Did anything sound good?"

She sipped of her watered-down honey whiskey. "Actually, I'm up for pretty much anything. I'm not a big shopper, though. So we could probably skip anything like that."

Before he could make another suggestion, Grace jumped up from her barstool and rushed away.

Blaze's face was red, and his brows were drawn tight.

His buddy was upset. No, he was *pissed.*

"What was that about?" Nick asked.

"I'm not entirely sure. But I'm determined to find out." Blaze slid from his seat and headed the same direction Grace had.

"What was that about?" Hope asked.

"I'm not sure." Nick glanced back at the bar, and his brother.

Charles wore a smug smile.

"I don't think it was something good, whatever our friends are fighting over." He watched his little brother down another drink.

"Nick?" Hope put her hand on his, bringing his attention back to her. "What're you thinking?"

He shook his head, trying to clear his mind. What was he going to do if his brother lost his shit?

He tried to focus on Hope, letting her hazel eyes draw him in. "Ah, nothing. So, L.A. sights, we can do that." He went back to planning their outing for the next day.

But when Charles left the bar in a rush, his eyes followed. He told himself to leave it at that and stay with his curvy brunette.

CHAPTER 7

Nick's little brother ripped Blaze and Grace apart, then slammed his fist into his buddy's face.

"Oh, shit!" Nick jumped up to fix whatever was going on.

Hope grabbed her purse and followed.

Both men were bloody by the time they made it to the veranda.

Hope went straight to Grace.

Nick tried to grab Charles, but his younger brother was slippery.

The boy slid around him, and went for Blaze again.

"You can't have her, she's mine!" Charles cried as he swung another fist.

"She's not something...you...can...own!" His bandmate yelled back and delivered a few of his own blows to Charles' abdomen.

His brother straightened and swung at Blaze again, but Nick's friend backed up just enough to miss the punch, and return a right cross.

With a sickening crack, Charles's nose broke and blood spurted.

Nick grabbed his still-struggling brother and pulled him a few feet from his friend.

"Hold him, Nick!" Blaze shouted. He came closer, his hands still in fists, ready to dish out a few more hits.

"Damn it! Stop, you two! This isn't high school!" Grace stepped in the way. She put one hand on both their chests, and took a deep breath, puffing it out. "Charles, how could you?"

He didn't look at her; his eyes were locked on Blaze, absolute fury burning in his hazel orbs. "Why do you have to take everything of mine?" He shouted over Grace's shoulder.

Nick shifted in front of her to block his brother, and looked down at the younger man, who was only a couple of inches shorter than him. "Dude, what're you talking about?" He got right in his brother's face.

"You and your stupid band; they took everything! Even the woman I love. It's never enough. He had to go and..." Charles wiped some of the blood off of his face and looked at Grace, now wrapped in Blaze's arms. "Why wasn't I enough for you? Not famous enough, not rich enough, not tough enough?" Charles didn't wait for an answer. He stormed off into the building.

The gathered crowd parted to make way for him.

Nick stayed right behind him.

♪

HOPE SCOWLED at the crowd of gawkers. "Show's over, get out of here!"

The crowd dispersed back into the ballroom.

Her friend was now wrapped in Blaze's arms. They needed alone time, so she retreated to the interior.

She looked around the ballroom for Nick and Charles. Didn't really expect to find them there, so she wandered out into the lobby and then outside.

Charles' voice was coming from around the corner of the building.

He didn't seem to be trying to be quiet. It was like he really didn't care who heard them.

Hope moved closer to eavesdrop.

"Why? You don't give a damn about me. You don't care! You never have!" Charles shouted.

"How can you say that?" Nick asked, and there was hurt in the question.

"It's true, and you know it! You were gone the whole time we were growing up. You care more about your precious *Razor's Edge* than you do about your own family."

"That's not true," Nick said, defensively.

"Really? Then why didn't you come to Barbara's funeral?" Charles accused.

"There's more to that and you know it," the elder brother said, and he sounded much calmer.

"You didn't love her. You didn't even come to say goodbye."

Tears filled Hope's eyes as she listened.

The brothers should be so close, yet there was so much tension.

Her heart broke for them.

"I loved her just as much as you. And you're right, I should've made it. I just...I couldn't deal with it, dude. How do you bury your little sister? It was my job to protect her, to protect all of you, and instead, I was flying around the world. I fucked up, okay? Is that what you want to hear? I feel guilty, but I can't change that. Barb knows how much I loved her. I dedicated the rest of my tour to her. What more do you want from me?"

"I want my big brother back." Charles's voice was barely above a whisper.

Hope peeked around the corner to see Nick pull Charles into a fierce hug. She smiled and snuck back into the hotel to wait.

She sat in the lobby for over an hour, Googling information

about Nick on her phone. She confirmed Barbara was his sister, who'd tragically died recently. Rumors indicated it was an accidental overdose of prescription medications.

Her heart broke all over again.

She'd lost her father recently, so Hope could feel what he was going through.

She was lucky; she didn't have the media judging her reaction. She'd read a book about grief a friend had given her, and everyone processed differently. Grief was private. No one else knew how much someone thought of their lost loved one or how they dealt with it.

If Nick wanted to tell her about it, Hope would listen, but she wouldn't mention it.

Sometimes someone just needs a break from grief, a reason to remember it was okay to be happy, and go on living.

Hope finally gave up on Nick coming back. She was disappointed, but he and Charles needed time to work things out.

Grace and Blaze were still on the balcony, so she headed back up to her room. She stopped at the front desk on her way back.

"Yes ma'am, how may I help you?" The young man behind the counter asked.

"I am staying in room 723. Could I have my friend pick up a key to my room? I'm not sure what time he'll be back, and I've got to get out of these shoes," Hope said.

The clerk smiled. "Of course, ma'am. What's his name?"

"Nick Ford." She waited for him to recognize the name, but he just made a note in the computer and smiled again.

"That's not a problem, Ms. Thatcher. I'm on duty all night so I'll make sure he gets it."

Hope thanked him and headed to her room. She sat on the bed to kick off her heels, then rubbed her feet before digging her phone out of her purse.

Nick had programmed his number into her contacts earlier and sent himself a text so he had her number, too.

. . .

HOPE: I hope everything's all right. There's a key to my room waiting for you at the front desk. If you need a break.

SHE TUCKED her phone into the top of her bra and pushed open the slider to the balcony.

The night air was cool and felt good.

Hope rolled her neck to loosen the tension and gazed out at the city lights. It was beautiful, but she still preferred being able to see the stars.

She stood outside for a while, then finally got ready for bed. She went into the bathroom to take off makeup. One look at the tub made Hope need a long soak. As soon as she pulled the pins from her hair, she could hear the *beep* of the keycard at the door.

He came back!

Nick stepped into the bathroom doorway and leaned against the jam.

Hope smiled and continued to take down her hair. "I'm glad you got my text," she said simply.

He looked so drained, and her heart skipped.

"Thanks for leaving a key," Nick whispered.

"Well," Hope said, breathless. "That was just wishful thinking on my part."

He half-smiled.

"I was going to have a bath. Would you care to join me?" she asked.

"Depends, are you gonna try to seduce me again?" he teased, the light returning to his blue eyes.

"Me? I thought you'd seduced me?" she smirked. Hope shook out her curls, leaving her hair a fluffy mess.

Nick stepped up behind her and unzipped her dress.

She held the material to her chest and faced him.

He leaned down, kissing her gently. His hands framed her face. Nick pulled back, his eyes searching her face. "That tub's gonna overflow if we don't get in soon."

She dropped her dress, and it fell to the floor with a *thump*.

"What was that?" Nick asked.

She burst out laughing.

"My phone. I stuck it in the top of my dress."

He chuckled and shook his head. "What am I gonna do with you?"

"I can think of lots of things you can do to me." Hope winked, torturing him. She stepped into the warm water and scooted to the back of the tub.

It was a little wider than an average tub, but it was extra-long. She could lay flat on her back with her feet on one end and head would barely reach the other end.

Nick quickly stripped down to join her. "Uh uh, scoot forward," he said.

"Why do you get the back?" she pouted. She slid forward and turned off the water as he stepped in behind her.

He pulled her back between his legs.

She rested her head against his chest.

"Cause then I can do this?" He ran his hands over her body, caressing her breasts.

She sighed and relaxed into him.

They sat in silence for a few minutes, letting the stress of the day drain away. Hope tilted her face to the left and looked at him. "How's Charles?"

"He'll be okay."

She waited for him to continue, not wanting to pressure him.

"I took him to the hospital. His nose is broken, but the doctor got him all packed up and I got him settled into a hotel near the airport. He's gonna go home for a while."

"Where do you live?" she asked, trying not to let the shock come across in her voice.

"Nashville. Most of the time."

Hope had been trying to avoid telling him she didn't live in L.A., but it didn't matter because *he* didn't either.

Tennessee.

That seemed so much farther away.

"Did you get things worked out with Charles?" she asked.

"Some of it, but there's been so much crap over the years, it's not gonna get fixed in one night." Nick sighed.

"You did the right thing," she said.

"Well, it's not gonna get better if we don't work on it. He needed to get away from Grace for a while, anyway."

Hope hated to ask, but she needed to know. "Are you flying back with him?" She tried to keep her voice light, but he saw right through that, and teased her.

"Why? You trying to get rid of me?"

She rolled over to look him in the eye. "I totally understand if you need to go. Families are forever. But would I be disappointed if I had to spend another couple of days with you?" She left the question hanging, as if she was debating the answer.

He tickled her, causing water to splash out of the tub.

They both broke down laughing.

"Come on," Hope said, standing up. "Let's go to bed."

Nick ducked his head under the water before standing up.

She handed him a towel, and they dried off.

When they hit the sheets, she curled up against him, enjoying the comfort of his arms, and quickly fell asleep.

CHAPTER 8

Hope waited with Nick and Blaze for Grace to finish her meeting at the new theater. Her bestie was about to take on a life-changing role.

It was nice to have the boys to entertain her in the meantime.

She was excited when Blaze picked them up at the hotel in a red Mustang convertible.

They walked around the Tar Pits looking at the sculptures.

Hope was wearing out.

Blaze checked his watch. "It's almost one. Grace said she'd meet us for lunch. Maybe we should head that way?"

"Sounds good! I'm starving!" she said.

She'd assumed they'd just head back to the hotel restaurant to wait for Grace, but Blaze drove them to an old movie theater called *The Majestic.*

It didn't look like it'd been a working theater in years. The front was covered with semi-clear plastic, torn in various places. The ancient-looking marquee had multiple busted light bulbs, but the name of the place was still visible.

"What're we doing here?" Nick asked.

"Picking Grace up. I thought we'd surprise her." The boybander wore a devilish grin.

Hope smiled back, conspiratorially.

The exterior of the theater gave the impression that renovations were slow-going.

She let her gaze roam.

Where is everyone? Or anyone?

All four sets of double doors were open, leading into the theater, and she pulled on Nick's arm, holding her breath, as they walked into the spacious auditorium. Hope went down to the front row and sat in the center seat.

Nick and Blaze followed, taking seats on either side of her.

"Oh, no!" She pushed them out of their seats. "I'm here to see a play, so go entertain me."

Her would-be man flashed a naughty smile and ran toward stage right.

She raised an eyebrow in Blaze's direction.

Both men took on her challenge, surprising her with their rendition of Romeo and Juliet.

They were pleasantly interrupted by Grace, which silenced Nick, who'd been playing Juliet.

Their performance ended with a round of applause from not only Hope, but two well-dressed men, and some of the construction crew.

Hope couldn't help but laugh at her best friend's reddened cheeks.

"Are you ready to go get lunch?" Grace asked.

"Not yet. Nick and I have one thing we need to do first," Blaze said.

Nick nodded and gestured to Hope. "Why don't you come up here, Hope? Grace, stay put!"

The guys exchanged a look, then Blaze sang.

"The moment I met you, my beauty, my life as I knew it, had changed.
You gave me your back, denied your broken heart,
Even it deserves a second chance.
Just a minute of your time, that's all I'm asking for,
to show you what you mean to me.

"Don't put us all together, not all men are created the same."
"Let me mend your broken heart, let me wipe your tears,
My life is tied to yours, we've waited all these years.
Let me mend your broken heart, let me wipe your tears.
My life is tied to yours, we've waited all these years."

THEY ENDED with an unbelievable harmonic tone.

Hope's heart raced with the speed on an Indy 500 car. She's never been serenaded before. And here was this hot, famous man, singing to her.

How did I get so lucky?

LUNCH WAS AMAZING. Blaze took them to a Chinese place he said he loved. Hope was so hungry, she didn't care where they ate.

The food was great; the conversation was… off.

Grace announced she was moving to L.A. permanently.

Hope was beyond excited for her best friend. It was a much-needed change in her life. Grace had lost her parents when they were teens and hadn't learned to move on. This would be good for her.

She was jealous, though. Hope would give anything for a major change in her boring life.

"I have to leave tomorrow morning. I'm rather quick at packing, it's the drive that's gonna kill me."

"Why don't you just get someone else to pack for you," Nick suggested.

If only I could help.

"I learned from a young age not to let someone else pack for you. Things get broken, or stolen. If I pack it and break it, it's my own damn fault."

"I can come with you and help you pack," Blaze said.

"Umm. No, you can't," Nick said. "Wednesday and Friday we're filming shows, remember? Ellen and Jimmy Kimmel? Management would kick your ass if you disappeared. The Ellen show is her once a year anything-goes live show. We can't *not* have you there."

"Dammit!" he cursed under his breath.

"It's okay, I'm better at packing when I'm alone, anyway. I just turn on some music and get it done.

"I really wish I could help, it took everything I could do to get the small amount of time off to come here now."

"I know, And I appreciate that," Grace said.

They headed back to the hotel where Blaze suggested meeting for dinner.

"Mind If I spend some more time with you?" Nick asked, pulling Hope off to the side, away from his buddy and her best friend.

"Oh, I'd love that." She could feel her cheeks heat.

They entered her room moments later; the door closing with a click.

Hope was nervous, and she didn't know why. Her palms were sweating as she clenched in and out of fists. She glanced toward the bathroom. She'd never be able to take a bath again without thinking about Nick's hands on her as they bathed together.

Her body was still deliciously sore.

He stepped up behind her and placed a chaste kiss on her neck.

It sent goosebumps rippling over her skin.

He leaned in closer, wrapping his arms around her waist, pulling her back to his chest. "There is nothing more I want to do," he whispered into her, "than make sweet love to you, again."

Her breath hitched. She tried to turn in his arms, but he held tight.

"But," he continued. "Please don't take this wrong."

Hope's stomach, full of wonderful food, lurched, his words hit her in the gut like a fist. "But...?"

"I'm so tired. Honey, you wear me out. Would you mind if we just curled up together and rested?"

Her entire body relaxed. She'd been so afraid he was going to say something like, 'thanks for the ride, but I gotta go,' or something to that nature. She wasn't expecting him to want to cuddle.

This time, when she tried to turn, Nick let her. She pushed to her tiptoes and kissed him softly. Once, twice, a third time. "A nap sounds wonderful."

He sat on the edge of the bed, then slipped off his shoes and socks.

Hope lowered the zipper on her jeans, but he stepped up to her.

"Baby, I really do want to just nap."

"I know." She frowned.

"Then, why are you getting naked?"

She laughed. "I don't know about you, but I can't nap in jeans. Too uncomfortable. I was going to put on pajama pants."

Nick's face brightened, and Hope couldn't help but smile.

"Do you sleep in your jeans?" she asked.

"Well, I don't normally nap. It doesn't fit into the schedule. But if I want to make it through dinner, I need sleep." Nick pulled her close, under the covers, her back fitting perfectly against his chest, her ass resting against his crotch.

She wanted him to do mind-blowing things to her, but her body was saying 'no, not right now'. She too, really needed sleep.

🎵

"SHIT! HOPE, WAKE UP!" Nick jumped out of bed, his heart slamming in his chest.

The clock was the only light in the room.

They'd slept for far too long.

"Dammit. We're supposed to meet Blaze and Grace in twenty minutes."

She yawned. "Yeah. So?"

He rushed around the room, snatching his jeans up and looking for his overshirt, feeling completely out of sorts. "We gotta get ready!"

"Nick. Breathe. Twenty minutes is plenty of time," she said, her voice still thick and groggy with sleep.

He paused his frantic movements, listening to her words and her tone. "It is?"

Hope nodded and climbed out of bed, getting ready faster than any woman he'd seen before..

Sure enough, less than twenty minutes later, they were ready and waiting in the lobby for their friends.

Dinner was uneventful, nothing more than the standard hotel bar and grill. However, when Blaze suggested his favorite karaoke bar, Hope's face lit up.

Not what Nick expected. "You'll sing, then?" he whispered in her ear.

"Of course. I love karaoke!"

He never could understand why his brother-from-another-mother loved the dive bar so much, Blaze dragged him there any time they were in town together.

They all laughed when Grace, unbeknownst to her—until afterwards—sang her heart out to a *Razor's Edge* song.

Hope had braved singing a *Pink* song she didn't know.

After being pushed by Grace, Nick relented, and sang his favorite song by *Journey*.

"Will you sing with me?" Hope asked after her third drink.

"Um, yeah? What song?" he asked.

"I kinda already put it in. I hope you know it."

Shit.

They called Nick and Hope up next. He held his breath waiting for the song title and lyrics to appear on the screen.

She'd chosen a song by *Kid Rock,* and *Sheryl Crow,* called, *Picture.*

He ran his hands through his hair as he belted out the heart-breaking lyrics. He was singing words true to him; his heart fully in the performance.

Hope's voice sounded as if it held the same heartache.

Their voices blended together so perfectly, like they'd been singing as a couple for years.

Nick slid an arm over her bare shoulders when they finished singing, and joined their friends back at the table.

The karaoke host called out the last song; it was for the whole crowd; everyone was to join in; *Closing Time* by *Semisonic.*

The entire bar sang, the sound a joyous one. Those who didn't know the verses had no problem catching on to the chorus.

They were still laughing, as they walked back to the hotel, arm-in-arm.

When they got into the lobby, Nick directed Hope to the elevator, hollering goodnight over his shoulder.

"Hope?" Grace called to his woman. "I won't get to see you in the morning."

The petite brunette slipped out from under his arm and headed back to her friend. "It was so good to see you! Thank you for everything! Call me tomorrow after you get settled, okay?"

They stepped back and peered at each other,

their eyes swimming with tears. Hope hugged Grace one more time before she joined Nick in the elevator.

He slipped his arm around her, ready to hold her while she cried. Surprise washed over him when no more tears fell.

They entered her hotel room and the moment the door was closed, she backed him against the wall.

"It was so hard keeping my hands to myself at the bar," Hope said, as she stood on her toes to kiss him. Her hands slipped under his T-shirt.

She was a little more forward than she'd been before. No idea where it was coming from, he was totally okay with it.

She had his shirt off before he could process any thought—with his big brain, anyways.

He matched her, piece of clothing, per piece of clothing. Soon, they stood there, both naked.

Nick shifted them around, pressing Hope up against the wall. He slid his hands down the sides of her body, catching her behind the knee. He encouraged her to wrap her legs around his waist.

He carried her back to the bed. Then knelt on the edge and laid her gently down. He let his mouth roam from hers to her delicate neck.

Her hands ran down his back as he moved slowly on, to tease her nipples with his tongue.

Hope's back arched, begging for more.

Nick kept moving, swirling his tongue around her belly button ring, and she gasped.

She moaned when he took in her most sensitive area.

The sound of her pleasure caused his cock to jerk. He stroked her with his tongue, taking his delight, and Hope cried out.

Her sex pulsed with climax.

He crawled back up her, placing himself between her soft thighs. Nick thrust into her.

She was hot, welcoming, and deep.

Their eyes met, and the unbridled passion in her eyes made him need to move faster.

Hope met him stroke for stroke, helping drive him deeper.

Right as his release crested, and he couldn't contain himself anymore, she orgasmed again, her core tightening around him. Nick lost control, exploding inside her.

She held him tight when he collapsed on top of her, ran her fingers through his hair when he nestled into her neck.

Their breathing slowed, and Nick was still inside her.

What the hell had just happened?

His previous lovers had always jumped up and run to the shower to wash off as soon as they finished.

Hope seemed content to lay here and hold him, and him hold her.

Why was that so comforting?

It seemed like such a girly thing to want to cuddle, but he did. Nick had always liked to cuddle afterward.

He looked up at Hope.

She had her eyes closed, and her beautiful face was flushed pink from their shared exertion. She glowed, and her beauty made his breath catch.

She seemed so content.

And…so was he?

CHAPTER 9

Nick awoke the next morning sprawled out on his side, covering Hope protectively with his body.

He'd insisted on sleeping on the right side of the bed because it was closest to the door.

He could hear her smooth rhythmic breathing. She was still asleep. He lay there a few minutes, reliving the night before.

Hope had let herself go with a reckless abandon and he'd enjoyed every minute. He hoped it meant she felt safe with him.

She stretched as she woke before she slid out from under him and walked naked into the bathroom.

Nick heard the sink running and could only guess what she was up to. When the shower started, every part of his body stirred.

He exited the warm bed and knocked on the bathroom door.

"Yeah?" he heard her call from the other side.

"Can I join you?" he asked, poking his head through the door.

She stuck her head out of the shower and looked at him suspiciously.

"I don't know... I'm naked in here and I'm not sure I know you well enough to have you see me naked," she teased.

"Oh, trust me. You know me well enough," Nick said, flashing what he thought was a seductive smile.

She ducked back behind the curtain.

He didn't wait for an official invitation. He stepped into the shower when she was rinsing her hair.

The small shower suddenly felt even smaller, with him towering over her. There was almost a foot difference in their height, but Nick didn't mind.

His hands slid around her wet body, pulling her against him for a kiss. Her lips were soft, and she tasted of mint toothpaste.

She wrapped her arms around his neck.

He took the opportunity to tickle her under her biceps.

She slipped back, letting the full spray of the shower hit him.

He jumped back out of the water. "Geez, what are you trying to do? Scald me?" he said, his eyes wide.

Hope laughed. "What's a matter too hot for you?"

"I knew you liked it hot, but, holy cow!"

She turned the temperature down a little and muttered that he was a big baby.

They switched places so he could wash off.

While he shampooed his hair, Hope lathered up a cloth with body wash and started rubbing it on his body. She started on his chest and worked her way down to his legs.

Hope knelt to wash his calves and feet. She made him turn and worked her way back up his back and arms.

When he turned back toward her, his erection bobbed a greeting.

"Are ya happy to see me?" Hope teased.

Nick didn't reply; he bent down and kissed her. His hands slid around her back and grabbed her butt. He lifted her up, wrapping her legs around him and pressed her against the side shower wall.

She held on tight when he thrust, then threw her head back in pleasure, driving him on further.

The hot water glided over them while they made love.

Nick's need was so urgent.

Her body spasmed around him, which pushed him over the edge.

He held her against the wall, both of them panting, and resting his forehead against her collarbone.

"Well that was unexpected," Hope said, with a giggle.

He looked up at her, searching for some kind of answer in her eyes.

"I don't know what you've done to me, but I just can't seem to get enough of you," he said.

She smiled and kissed him softly. "How was I lucky enough to find you?"

He set her back on my feet. "I'm the lucky one," he whispered.

When Hope didn't answer, he met her eyes and flashed another smile, wondering what she was thinking.

"What are your plans for today?" Nick inquired.

"I, um. I don't know. I'm supposed to spend the next few days with Grace, but as we know, that changed. I'm really excited for her, but I miss her already."

He nodded. "Let's go get something to eat and do some shopping. You're spending those days with me." Somehow, it just felt so natural for them to do things as a couple. They'd only known each other two days.

🎵

NICK AND HOPE had lunch at the Monsoon Café, an elegant Asian restaurant.

"I'm impressed you can eat with chopsticks, most people can't." He laughed at the face she made when he ordered sushi. "You don't like sushi?" he asked.

"If I'm paying this much for fish, they damn well better cook it," she said.

He laughed loud enough to draw the attention of some people around them. "You're so funny," he teased.

"I know, but looks aren't everything."

He laughed more. "So, I have a thing tomorrow, with *Razor's Edge*. And I'd like you to join me."

"Oh, um, okay? Do I need to dress nicely? Because I'm down to just my touristy clothes."

"After lunch, let's go shopping downtown."

While Hope explored the ladies' section, Nick took off to get a royal blue silk shirt. She was looking through racks of dresses when he returned. "How's it going?"

She rolled her eyes, sure her irritation was apparent on her face. "I hate shopping for clothes, Can't ever tell how something on a hanger would look on."

"Everything will look good on you. Mind if I help?"

"You don't have to. I'm sure you could find a million things you'd rather do than help me find a dress," she pointed out.

He chuckled. "I grew up with three sisters. This will be a piece of cake."

She wasn't convinced but was willing to try.

Within twenty minutes, Hope had an arm-load of dresses to try on.

Nick followed her to the dressing room.

"I want to see them all," he said.

After trying on almost every dress and all of them being rejected by Nick—whom Hope had declared would now be known as Mr. Picky—she put on a strapless royal blue and black dress and stepped out of the dressing room.

The dress was a basic black slip that stopped to mid-thigh and had a second layer of blue material that looked like someone had drawn vertical squiggles running down it.

She was surprised to see that Blaze had joined Nick.

"Well?" she asked, getting their attention.

Blaze wolf-whistled, and it made Hope smile.

Nick cleared his throat and looked a little uncomfortable. "Yeah, that's it. That's the one."

She headed back to the dressing room. Why had Nick reacted like that? He'd seen her in a lot less than this dress.

Hope changed back into her jeans and pink V-neck T-shirt, then stepped out to meet the guys.

"Hey babe, Blaze is gonna keep you company while I run an errand. I'll meet you back at your hotel room before the event, okay?" Nick said.

"Sure," she said.

"Oh, here." He handed Hope his credit card.

"What's this for?"

"For the dress."

"Nick! You're not buying me a dress. I'm quite capable of paying for my own clothes." Hope stuffed the card in his jeans pocket.

"But I meant to buy it for you. It's just that I got to be somewhere, soon."

"That's very sweet of you, but I'm a big girl. Now, get outta here and I'll see you tonight."

She kissed him goodbye and watched his ass as he walked out of sight.

Blaze followed her to the check-out. He then led her out to a quant street café for coffee. "Pretty impressive," he said, after they sat down with their drinks.

"What's impressive?"

"That you wouldn't let him pay."

"Well, it's my dress. It doesn't make sense for him to buy it."

"It's just... well... not how most girls would react. After all, he did spend $5000 to dance with Grace."

"Yeah, well there's still no reason he should pay for my dress. Besides, that money went to a good cause. Those kids need some positive influences in their lives. So, speaking of Grace..."

"I think I love her. Damn. I can't believe I said that. Please don't repeat that."

Hope giggled. "I won't. It's not my place to share something that intimate. But, have you heard from her yet?"

As if it was fated, Blaze's phone *pinged*. He picked up and chuckled. "She landed."

"Oh, good. Um, I should ask, since you're the only other member of *Razor's Edge* I know, is it really all right that Nick invited me to… well, I'm not even sure what he invited me to."

"I can tell you, he didn't ask me, or the others, but I'd be honored for you to be there. Speaking of which, we have rehearsals in less than an hour. Should we head back to the hotel so you can drop off your things?"

An hour later, Hope walked with Blaze into a studio.

Nick was still nowhere to be seen.

She looked around and where they were sunk in. It was a TV studio. A production crew member met them at the door.

"Mr. Solan, if you'll follow me, the rest of the band is over here."

"Nick?" Hope whispered.

Blaze shrugged.

"BJ! You're here!" A tall, thin, blonde woman ran toward them, stopping only when she got right in front of the dark-haired man. "I was so worried. You aren't normally late like this." She looked over at Hope, a sneer across her face. "And who is this?" Her tone said everything her words didn't.

Hope tried not to cringe at the beautiful woman's voice.

Blaze slipped his arm around the petite's woman's shoulders, pulling her close. "This, dear Ronnie, is Hope. Nick's girl. Be nice to her, or you'll have to deal with me."

The blonde's attitude changed. As did her body language. "Oh, I'm so sorry, sweetie! We get so many freaks that sneak in here, I never know who belongs and who doesn't."

"She belongs. That's all that matters. So, where are we set up?"

Ronnie led the way, at least ten steps ahead of them, giving Hope a chance to speak privately with Blaze. "Why did she call you BJ? And who is she?"

"Oh, yeah. I forgot you don't know us for *Razor's Edge*. That just doesn't happen in our lives. Well, um, the fans know me as BJ. Only close friends call me Blaze. And Ronnie, she's one of our makeup artists. She's a little rough around the edges but has a good heart. Come on, let me introduce you to the band."

Hope tried to calm her nerves when her bestie's boy took her to meet the members of *Razor's Edge*.

"This is Dwaine," he introduced the shortest of the men.

A handsome guy that looked Hispanic. Maybe Puerto Rican?

"Hi! How you doin'?"

She giggled. "I'm well, thank you."

"Scoot over," an adorable blond man said, shoving Dwaine out of the way. He reached for Hope's hand. "Never fear." He kissed her knuckles. "Thomas is here."

Hope glanced at Blaze, who looked like he was trying hard not to laugh.

"Bro, Nick's standing behind you with murderous intent on his face. You might want to let his girl go."

Her man stepped around Thomas, opening his arms to Hope, asking her to come, without saying a word.

She stepped into his embrace.

He held her tight.

Too tight.

"Nick." She pushed back just enough to be able to look up at him. "What's wrong?"

"Nothing. I just needed to check on my brother. He infuriates me. I'm good."

"Are you going to hold on to her forever, or do I get to be introduced?" The voice behind her was smooth, deep, and far too sexy.

Nick released her and turned her around. "Hope, I'd like you to meet Scott. The big brother of our group. He just came back, after taking a few years off."

Scott didn't wait for an invitation; he just pulled her straight into a deep hug. "Welcome to the family," he whispered in her ear.

Welcome to the family?

Does he know something I don't know?

"Boys! Let's go!" A woman with a headset called and gestured.

"Honey, you can sit over here," Nick said, leading her over to the side.

CHAPTER 10

Hope had never seen anything like this in her life.

Five men with perfect harmony, in sync with each other's movements, absolutely professional.

That was, until they finished rehearsing. Then, they were five brothers, laughing and teasing each other like children.

It was amazing to see the comradery they shared; the family values they had for each other. It reminded Hope of her and Grace, when they had done their first and only play together. It made her miss her friend. However, she was excited to hear what the future held for the tall chestnut-haired beauty.

After three hours of rehearsing, Nick came to her, sweating and exhausted. He leaned down to plant a wet kiss on her cheek. "Hopefully, we only have a few more run-throughs, then we can head out of here. I'm fucking beat."

"I bet."

Where would they head? Should she ask? As it was, she'd had no clue rehearsal was what Nick had wanted to bring her to.

Why did he want me here? To see what he does, to brag?

She shook her head when he walked away, banishing the absurd thought. Hope still couldn't wrap her head around why he wanted to spend time with her at all, let alone bring her to the filming of a TV show he was going to be on.

It was a foreign feeling.

She rarely felt wanted.

He made her feel even more than just wanted.

Desired, cherished, loved.

What?

Love... no.

She pushed that away, too. They'd met *four* days ago.

What was going on between them? Everything in the last few days had been overwhelming.

She'd come to L.A. to see her best friend. That was all.

Then she'd met Nick.

That could have... no, *should* have been a one-night stand.

He wasn't the type of guy that looked at her, let alone spent a night with her. She never would've thought to ask for more.

Why should she?

He was a tall, hot, famous rockstar who traveled the world, singing to thousands of beautiful women every night.

She was a short, curvy girl who'd only been to three states in her whole life and spent her free time in jeans and boots, mucking horse shit.

What could they possibly have in common?

Yet, he was there with her, bringing her to meet his family.

They might not be blood, but it was clear they were a family. They'd welcomed her.

Her only real concern was their sexual habits. He made her so hot and crazy, she didn't think about protection until it was too late. She was on birth control, but he'd possibly been with hundreds of women. She needed to insist they pick up some condoms.

Hope swallowed when Nick came back a short time later, offered her his hand, and pulled her to her feet.

"Are you ready to go?"

She just nodded.

"Okay. I could use a shower and I'm starving. Blaze is gonna give us a ride back to the hotel. If it's all right, I'd rather stay with you again. I think he's gonna mope about and complain about missing Grace."

She laughed. She understood that. Her dear friend had seemed to leave a mark on people wherever she went.

It wasn't intentional. Grace just had something about her that drew people in.

Grace had always been the outgoing one in their friendship, where Hope was the one that simply was along for the ride. She wasn't adventurous, or wild. Just a simple country girl.

Nick had had a day. All he wanted to do was spend it with Hope, getting down to all the little things about her he didn't know yet.

As he stood in the hot shower, letting the water wash away his day, he contemplated all the things he *did* know about his little dark-haired beauty.

She had a big heart. He'd seen it in the way she handled not only his brother at the masquerade, but how she'd been with Blaze.

She was beautiful in a way most others were not.

She didn't see the beauty she held. It wasn't just the baby softness of her chocolate hair or the olive tone in her perfect skin. Nor was it the fact that her ass had just the right amount of plump to it to cause his cock to harden, or her cherry nipples that begged to be suckled.

It was more than that.

He couldn't put it into words.

Nick had had more than his share of lovers over the years.

Hell, he'd been with the band since he was twelve. RE was all he'd known.

Hope was nothing like the others. Everything he needed.

He didn't care if there'd be backlash over desiring a girl with some meat on her bones. He was sick of dating girls with no meat on their thighs because it was expected of him.

Damn the media to hell for choosing who he should date. This time, *he'd* made his decision. To hell with anyone that didn't agree.

The water was turning his fingers to raisins, and all he could think about was shouting out to the world, he wanted this woman.

His body was alive with the thought of her.

Nick stepped out of the shower, wrapped the towel around his waist, not caring that his hair was still dripping wet, and stepped into the other room.

He wanted her, needed her.

She was asleep.

He gazed at her for a few minutes; couldn't really be upset. He'd kept her awake most of the previous night, after all.

Nick dressed silently before picking up the phone to order food. He was starving but didn't want to wake her.

It was dinner time, but waffles, eggs, and bacon sounded really good to him.

Less than thirty minutes later, the knock at the door awoke his sleeping beauty.

"Is that bacon I smell?" Hope asked, the sleep making her voice raspy.

"It is. And waffles. I hope you're hungry."

"Starving."

She stretched like a cat, flexing all her muscles before climbing off the bed and joining him at the small table under the window. "I'm sorry I fell asleep. I didn't mean to."

Nick chuckled. "It's okay. I almost curled up next to you. But I needed food more than sleep. It doesn't help, I took an hour-long shower. I kept hoping you'd come join me."

Her cheeks flushed with color. He loved that about her.

"I, well. I thought you'd be too tired for extracurricular activities. Guess I was the one that was too tired." Hope picked up a piece of bacon and took the smallest of bites.

He watched her face; her eyes were intense.

She was debating something.

But what? It made his stomach twist in knots.

"Nick, why am I here?" she asked, her voice low and sincere.

He frowned. "Don't you want to be?"

"I do, it's just..." Her cheeks went even redder, and she wouldn't look at him.

"Just what?" He tilted her chin up so she'd have to.

"You're famous. Lots of people look up to you and I'm nobody," she said, dropping her hands and eyes to her lap again.

"Hope."

She didn't respond.

"Look at me." Nick waited until she did so. "You're *not* nobody. You're the first girl in, I don't know how long, that hasn't treated me like I'm famous. You don't see me as a guy from *Razor's Edge*. You just treat me like a normal man. Do you know how rare that is for me?"

"Don't you like being famous?" she asked.

He shrugged. "I love what I do. I love singing and I love my brothers, I even love every one of our fans, but what I want is someone who *gets* me." He ran his hand across her cheek and up into her hair. "Your eyes are really green," he said, cocking his head to one side.

She smiled conspiratorially.

"I could've sworn they were hazel, a mix of brown and green," Nick said.

"They're hazel, but they get more green for two reasons, and this time, I'm not crying," she said.

He smiled and leaned in, kissing her tenderly.

Her lips were soft and yielding under his.

He parted them, and gently caressed her tongue with his. Nick broke their kiss and took the bacon from her, setting it on the table. He stood and held a hand out

She hesitated a moment before taking it.

He pulled her to her feet and led her back to the bed.

Hope faced the bed, and he came up behind her, wrapping his right arm around her waist, pushing the hair away from the back of her neck so he could place a soft kiss with his free one.

She shivered.

He moved to the side of her neck and the top of her shoulder. Nick found his way to the zipper of her dress, and pulled it slowly down.

Hope's breathing became pants.

He let the fabric fall to her waist.

She wasn't wearing a bra; her back was smooth.

He ran his fingers over the soft skin down to push the skirt off her hips, revealing the blue lacy panties.

He whirled her around, and took in the sight of her bare breasts. The perfect cherry nipples called to him. His cock pressed against the rough fabric of his jeans.

Hope reached for the buttons on his dress-shirt. She seemed disappointed to find him wearing a tank top underneath.

He pulled off both shirts and dropped them to the floor. Nick returned quickly, unable to keep his hands to himself. He had to touch her...everywhere.

Hope ran hers up his chest as he pulled her in for a kiss. Her touch glided up behind his neck, pressing her warm body to his.

Nick groaned at the feel of her. He encircled her as he kissed her deeply. He gripped her firm, round behind as he ground her against him.

She trailed her fingertips down his arms and looped hers inside his.

Nick was barely aware of what she'd done before she had his buckle undone.

She unbuttoned his pants to free him and began to stroke.

He grunted and kissed her harder.

Hope pushed his pants down. She still had her heels on.

He pulled one leg up and kissed the inside of her ankle, then pulled her shoe off. He kept kissing her there, moving up her calf to the inside of her knee.

She whimpered in anticipation.

Nick got halfway up her thigh, then moved to the other leg.

She moaned in dissatisfaction at being led to the brink then made to wait again.

He smiled; that was exactly the reaction he'd wanted. He kissed his way up her other leg.

She writhed beneath him.

Nick pulled off the lacy panties, and pushed her legs apart to allow him access. He gently flicked his tongue against her, bringing out a gasp from deep inside her.

He smiled to himself, he wanted her, *all* of her, but he was going to take his time and enjoy this.

He licked and suckled her, torturing her blissfully until Hope came, crying out.

Nick crawled up next to her, watching her body shake with the aftershocks.

When she regained control, she rolled up next to him, pressing the length of her body against his. "Two can play that game," she whispered huskily.

Hope kissed her way down his body.

He sucked in a breath when she took him into her mouth.

She worked him slowly at first, swirling her tongue around his tip.

Nick shuddered in pleasure, but it wasn't until she started humming that he almost lost his restraint.

He couldn't hold back any longer, he pulled her up and

flipped them over so he was on top of her. He didn't want to come with her mouth on him. He wanted to come inside her.

She wrapped her legs around him and Nick plunged deep.

They both gasped.

He kept a rapid pace, covering them both in a sheen of sweat.

Hope shook, and her body spasmed around him.

He thrust as far as he could go, and held on as his body exploded.

They both lay paralyzed by the orgasms flowing through them.

Eventually, Nick collapsed into her. He relished the feeling. There was nothing more calming or comforting than the feel of his body covering Hope's, protecting her.

He rose onto his elbows and kissed her. When he started to get up, her legs were still wrapped around him.

"Where do you think you're going?" she smiled.

"I just thought you'd like to clean up."

"You thought wrong. I like the smell of you all over me. But we really should get something, if we are going to keep going at it like rabbits."

Nick smiled and relaxed back onto her with a sigh.

Yeah, he'd been right before.

She really was special.

CHAPTER 11

"It's the *Ellen* show? You didn't tell me it was *Ellen!*" Panic inched up Hope's spine and she had to pant a little bit. Sure, the band was going to be on a TV show, but *Ellen* was one of her favorites.

"I didn't know it mattered," Nick said.

"Yeah. It does," she whispered. "I'm nervous."

He chuckled. "You're hanging out with the men in the world's most popular pop band, and you're nervous to meet Ellen?"

"So?"

"So, that's cute. And kinda hurts my feelings."

Her already-knotted stomach lurched. She'd never want to hurt him. However, one look into his intense blue eyes told her he'd been teasing. She hit his chest with a loud, *smack.*

He mock-winced and swatted her hand away, with a wink. "I'll make introductions after the show. You stand right here. I gotta get over there." Nick left her off to the side of the stage, and rushed to join his brothers behind the scenes.

Her heart raced as the show began.

"I'm Ellen. But you already knew that. I can't wait to tell you about my guests for the day. The awesome band, *Razor's Edge.* Once a year, I do a live show so people can see how hard it really is hosting a talk show." The hostess introduced the band.

Thomas was a goofball, as Hope had gotten the impression he would be, after their first meeting.

Dwaine announced he was about to be a daddy again.

Scott talked about being glad to return to his brothers after taking a break to 'reflect,' whatever that meant.

Then Ellen turned to Blaze.

"What have I been up to lately? Well, I fell in love."

Hope had had a feeling that was coming. She was so elated for her best friend.

"I miss you, and I just want you to know, I'll never break your heart. I love you," her bestie's man continued.

Nick smacked the man across the chest. "Dude, not cool. I was going to talk about how *I* fell in love."

Hope's heart skipped a beat. Her knees wobbled.

What?!

Maybe I should sit.

Before she fell on her ass.

Hope was sure it was all for show, that Nick needed to up-stage his friend. There was no way he could mean it. This couldn't be real, could it?

Ellen, the comedian she was, jumped right in. "And your fans are okay with the two of you falling in love with each other?"

Nick stuttered and turned bright red. He pointed to Hope. "A girl, I promise! I fell in love with a girl. She's standing right over there."

A cameraman swung his equipment her way.

Her cheeks seared. She was going to be on TV!

Ellen saved her. "Well, then. I think it's time to hear if these boys still have it going on. So, what're you going to sing?"

"We're gonna treat ya'll to something from our new album, a song called *Peach*," Scott announced.

When the song was over, they cut to a commercial break.

Nick ran to Hope's side.

He leaned in for a kiss, but she pulled away.

"What?" he asked.

"You're in so much trouble, mister." She tried to use her best schoolteacher voice.

"Why?" He reared back, his mouth hanging half-open.

"Because of…" she twirled her finger at the stage, where the guys had been sitting for the interview.

Nick chuckled. "Ah, come on, baby. You know how I feel about you; I mean after last night…" He waggled his eyebrows at her.

Hope smacked him.

The night before had been amazing, and she was falling for him, but National Television?

Really?

He quickly kissed her cheek and ran back, because the commercial break was over.

"Welcome back!" Ellen said. "In case you just tuned in, today we have *Razor's Edge* with us."

The screams were almost deafening.

Hope studied each of the guys' reactions.

They all seemed so grateful to have their fans, and were humbled by the love of the crowd.

Ellen asked the guys if they wanted to play a game.

After the crowd screamed in excitement, the band agreed.

Ellen explained the game.

Hope hadn't been listening to the hostess, she was too busy visually stalking Nick.

Then she heard the screaming, and it plugged her back in.

"Well, it looks like we have some volunteers," Ellen said. "I think it's only fair that the guys pick their partners for this game."

More cheers went up.

The girls were jumping up and down trying to get their attention.

As four of the guys walked into the audience, Ellen grabbed Nick's jacket and pointed at Hope.

He got a devilish grin and headed straight for her.

She backed away, trying to find an escape, but the stagehands had been watching and pushed her back towards her man.

Nick took her hand and led her out on stage.

She was shaking so badly her teeth chattered.

"It's okay," he whispered. "It's just a game."

Hope stood next to him, shaking; petrified.

The girls around her were all fawning over the other guys.

She tried to focus on them, to forget the nerves swimming in her gut.

"Okay, the object of the game is to get five oranges into your baskets," Ellen explained. "The girls will give you the orange, you have to carry it over to the basket and drop it in. The first team to get five oranges in, wins. Now, the catch is, you can't use your hands."

Of course, there was going to be a catch.

"The girls will hold the orange like this," the hostess put the orange between her chin and chest.

A cheer went up from the audience.

"The guys have to remove the orange, holding it the same way and carry it to their basket. If you drop it, you have to go back for another."

Hope met Nick's eyes.

He was smiling.

She tried to relax.

What was the worst that could happen; they'd drop the orange?

Who cares?

Nick leaned in. "Think Grace will give us a bad time if we win?"

"She'll give me a bad time, anyway," Hope said.

"Okay, girls! Grab an orange," Ellen called.

All the girls tucked an orange under their chins as they stood in a line with the guys in front of them.

"Go!" Ellen yelled.

Nick leaned down and hooked the orange under her chin. He lifted it out and made his way over to the basket.

He wasn't in the lead. How? That'd been so fast!

She tucked another orange under her chin and waited.

He returned after successfully dropping it in the basket. Nick took the second one, but it fell to the floor as they were passing it.

Hope picked it up and put it back under her chin, and he took it smoothly this time.

Although he appeared to be hurrying, he wasn't. It was almost like he was trying to lose, if not by much.

Dwaine was dropping his third orange in the basket when Nick returned to take their third one.

"You'd better hustle," she whispered as he took it the next one.

Nick pulled away and winked. He was headed back for the fifth orange when Scott dropped his fifth in the basket.

"We have a winner!" Ellen yelled.

The TV hostess took both Scott and his girl's hand and held them in the air.

Everyone applauded.

She awarded the winner her prize, an iPad, before cutting to commercial.

Hope tried to head backstage, but Ellen asked all the girls to stay there.

Nick leaned close again . "Now aren't you glad we didn't win?" His tone was sly.

"You did that on purpose," Hope said, frowning.

"I have no idea what you're talking about," he said, those blue eyes wide with innocence.

HOPE LAY CURLED IN BED, her head resting on Nick's hard chest.

They were both exhausted after their excursions that day; which included a fabulous lovemaking session once they'd returned from *The Ellen Show*.

She wanted to talk about his declaration, but she was so tired.

They *needed* to talk about it though.

It can wait until the morning. Best to do it right before I hop on my plane.

Hope was almost asleep when she heard the buzzing of Nick's cellphone on the nightstand.

He ignored it, as did she. He continued to receive texts for the next fifteen minutes.

"Baby, why don't you just check that? It could be something important," she whispered.

He let out a moan. "I don't wanna move. But you're right. They're persistent, so it might be."

Hope hadn't called Grace after the show. She'd been so wrapped up in Nick and what'd happened during the day, she'd completely spaced out calling her friend. Blaze had made a declaration, too.

She sat up so that Nick could reach his phone, then turned the nightstand beside her. She grabbed her own cell from the charger cord.

There were no missed calls and no messages from Grace. Hope wasn't really worried though. Her bestie had a lot to do in only a few days and probably hadn't had time.

"Hey baby, have you heard from Grace?" Nick asked.

She glanced over her shoulder; he was still looking down at his phone. "No, I haven't, why?" She didn't like the odd sound in Nick's voice.

"Blaze sent me fifteen text messages. He can't get a hold of her, and he's freaking out."

"Tell him to get a hold of himself and go to bed. Grace turns off the ringer at about nine p.m. I'm sure she's already passed out at this point. She had a busy day, too."

He spoke out loud, slowly, while he typed out his reply. "Hope says get your panties out of a bunch. Grace is probably asleep. Try again in the morning. Shutting my phone off now."

CHAPTER 12

Bright rays of sunlight filtered in the room through a slit in the curtains. Nick stretched all his muscles, enjoying the ache in his body.

It was well earned.

He glanced over at the woman sleeping beside him. Their time was limited. She'd be leaving soon. Too soon.

Nick wanted to push the strand of hair off of her face but was afraid he'd wake her. Instead, he watched her sleep, her breathing deep and peaceful.

She was like no other woman he'd ever had in his bed.

He had to say goodbye.

But for how long?

They'd be in L.A. for a few weeks, then off to Chicago, followed by a nine-month tour. If he was lucky, he'd see her at a show if there was one in her town. Would that be enough?

One night with her?

It's better than nothing.

He slid off the bed and headed to the shower. Nick needed to clear his head.

"Baby, I hate to wake you up, but I don't know what time your flight is," Nick whispered in Hope's ear about ten minutes later.

She'd mentioned the day before her flight was late morning, but he didn't know more than that.

Hope yawned, rubbing at her eyes. "It's at eleven. What time is it now?" She rolled over to look at the clock and jumped out of bed. "It's after nine! Why didn't you wake me?"

Nick watched, helplessness washing over him, as she flitted about the room, throwing things in her suitcase before rushing to the bathroom. "Babe, are you all right?"

She rushed into the shower. "Yes. Uh, no. I, um, I get massive anxiety about getting to the airport on time."

"We've got plenty of time. It only takes about fifteen minutes from here." He struggled to understand how she could be this much of a wreck over getting to the airport.

"I still have to check my bag, get my boarding pass, and get through security."

What could he say to make her feel better? "Is there, uh, anything I can do?"

"No. I just need to hurry."

This wasn't how Nick had planned his final moments with her, but what could he do?

Twenty minutes later, they were heading to the parking garage.

"What're we doing here? I thought the cabbies picked you up out front?" she asked.

"Yeah, but my car's parked down here."

Hope cocked an eyebrow. "You have a car here?"

"Yeah?"

"Then why has Blaze been driving us around?"

Nick laughed. "I like making him be my chauffeur."

They walked over to a beautiful black Beemer with dark-tinted windows.

He popped the trunk and put her suitcase in, slamming it with a finality he didn't like.

Soon, they were rushing toward the airport.

"You didn't have to take me, you know," Hope said. "I could've gotten a cab."

He dared to take his eye off the road long enough for a glimpse at her. He couldn't help but notice red-rimmed eyes. "I wouldn't miss seeing you off for anything." Nick grabbed her hand and kissed her knuckles. He could tell something was on her mind, but he wouldn't push.

If she wanted to talk, she'd speak up.

The ride to the airport seemed to rush by for him.

Hope, on the other hand, seemed to be counting each second.

"What airline?" he asked.

"Delta, but you can just drop me off…"

"I don't think so." Nick pulled into the short-term parking and into the first available spot. He'd turned the engine off and gotten out of the car before she spoke again.

"You don't have to come with me, we could say goodbye here."

"Hope, are you trying to get rid of me?" His words brought forth the tears he'd suspected she'd been holding back.

"No! I just…I still don't understand all this. Your attention to me, your declaration. Especially the way you made it…I'm still confused."

He grabbed the handle of her suitcase and led her inside. How the hell should he reply? Hadn't he done a well enough job of showing how he felt?

Nick's declaration had been totally spontaneous.

He hadn't meant to do it. It'd just happened.

That didn't mean he hadn't meant what he'd said.

They reached the ticket counter, and Hope stepped forward to check-in.

Nick's phone rang.

Damn it.

He ignored it, but when it rang again, he pulled it out of his pocket.

Blaze.

He can wait.

Nick shoved the cell back in his pocket, not wanting anything to take time away from Hope.

"Glad that's done. Now for security," she said.

He slipped his hand into hers, not waiting for an invitation. He wasn't going to let her go until he absolutely had to.

They hadn't talked about what would happen next.

I guess it'll have to wait until we talk on the phone tonight.

At the entrance to the security line, Nick pulled her off to the side and into his arms. "You'll call me as soon as you land?"

"If you want me to."

He let out a huff. He wanted to come back with a snarky, *duh*, but didn't want to be an ass in their last moments.

Instead, he kissed the top of her head.

She made eye contact, hers filled with so much turmoil.

He took that moment to capture her lips, telling her everything he couldn't form into words. Nick didn't care if people stared.

He was where he needed to be, doing what he needed to do.

Hope kissed him back with the same fire, and it calmed his soul.

"I'll let you know when I get to my gate," she said, pushing softly against his chest.

He reluctantly released her, in more ways than one. He kept his gaze on her until she was no longer in sight. Nick let out the breath he didn't know he was holding, turned, and headed for his car.

Buzz, buzz went his phone again. He glanced at the screen.

Blaze, again.

He accepted the call and let out a grunt.

"Hey, Nick, I know you're about to take Hope to the airport, but I need some help."

"I already did. What's up, bro?" he asked and started his car.

"I've been patiently waiting for Grace to call me back. I quit calling her, but I sent her another text. I got a reply while I was in the shower. *'Leave me alone. I don't want you anymore'.*"

"Seriously?"

"I don't get it, I thought she'd be happy I told everyone—the whole freaking world—I was in love with her. Don't chicks normally dig that?"

Nick laughed. "Yeah, sure, but Grace is different from anyone you've ever dated. If you're really concerned, I'll see what Hope thinks. Call you back in a few." He disconnected the call and selected Hope.

"I'm getting on the plane," she said by way of answer.

"Just a quick question. It's about Grace."

🎼♫

"Hope had already boarded when you called," Nick said as the car sped down the highway. "She said it doesn't sound like Grace. She said if Grace has a problem with you, she'd tell you to your face, or at least over the phone. Hope's certain she wouldn't send a text like that."

Blaze sighed. "Not that I'd ever call Hope a liar, but this came from Grace's number. So unless someone's there with her, she sent it."

"Hope said she'd try to call Grace. See if she can find out what's going on. She'll call me back as soon as she lands."

"I tried calling after I got the message. It went straight to voicemail. Did Hope say she had a landline?" The frustration in his voice was obvious.

"She didn't. But if you can't wait the three hours for her to land in Pasco, there's someone who'd know how to get a hold of her."

"Yeah, her boss. I don't know why I didn't think of him first," Blaze said.

"Good idea, but not who I was thinking."

"Who?"

"My brother. They spent five months together. Not together-together, but you know what I mean." When his friend didn't answer, he regretted saying that. Nick switched gears. "I think you're right, Blaze. I'll pick you up and go to the theater with you. They can at least tell us if they've heard from her."

CHAPTER 13

They got no help at the theater.

Nick tried calling his brother on the way back to Blaze's place, but only got his voicemail.

He slid onto the brown leather sofa in the living room, watching his buddy pace.

Their open beers sat untouched on the coffee table.

"You can't get a hold of your brother. I can't get a hold of Grace. Hope says something isn't right. Are you fucking kidding me?" Blaze stopped his jerky movements long enough to pick up his drink. He brought it to his lips but never took a sip. "He's obsessed with her. Remember our fight?" He raged, setting the warming bottle back down, then falling back into pacing.

"I know…" Nick completely understood his frustration.

"I have to do something."

"We have obligations," he reminded his bandmate. "You can't miss the *Jimmy Kimmel* taping. Besides, you don't know something's wrong."

"Fuck that, man. This is *Grace*. Answer me honestly. Would he hurt her?"

Nick cursed. "I don't know…" he whispered.

"Look, I know he's your brother, but she's my…"

He could hear the hopelessness in Blaze's voice, and when they made eye contact, Nick could feel it. "I don't know what he's capable of, but I know he thinks he actually loves her."

"One thing I learned from Grace; everyone sees love a little differently. The difference is, how to show it."

His cell rang. "Shit, it's Angel." He put the phone on speaker. "Hey, sis."

"Nicky? Did you ever get a hold of Charles? I'm getting worried."

Nick snapped his head up, meeting his buddy's eyes again. "No."

"Oh. Well, damn."

"Angel. What's up…" he prompted.

"He was acting all funny. I don't know, like he was high or something. He wasn't. I can always tell when he's fallen off the wagon, and this isn't it. He just kept walking around the house, in a constant circle, mumbling something about roses."

"Did he say anything else, before he left?" Nick pushed.

"I didn't even know he'd left! When I went to bed, he was still leaving tracks on the kitchen floor. I woke up about nine a.m. and he was gone. No note, no goodbye. Nothing. Nicky, and I'm worried. You don't think he's relapsing, do you?"

He sighed. "I don't think this is drugs. But keep trying to get a hold of him. And let me know if you do." He set his phone on the couch after disconnecting .

"That's it. I have to get to her. I need to get to Denver."

Nick stepped right up to Blaze, putting his hands on his shoulders, hoping to ground him. "Try and get some sleep. There's nothing you can do tonight. Tomorrow we can try again to reach Grace's bosses and see what they know. If it comes down to it, we can fly out tomorrow night, together. Just slow down, dude." He grabbed his phone and headed for the front door. "I'll call you in the morning."

NICK CRAWLED INTO BED, absolutely exhausted. It'd been the craziest couple of days he'd ever experienced. He'd grown up on crazy, so that was saying something.

Hope had called, letting him know she was home safe. She'd claimed she didn't have a lot of time to chat; she had chores to do. Something about a horse and a field.

He didn't press. She'd had a long week, too.

What was going on in her mind?

Then there was Blaze, worrying them both about Grace.

"Hope will call me if she needs me," he said to himself when he turned out the lights.

Nick had to be up at oh-dark-thirty for their rehearsal before *the Jimmy Kimmel Show*. They didn't get the luxury they'd had for Ellen's taping. It was two run-throughs, then taping. It would be another long day.

With only a few hours of sleep, he relished the coffee he sipped while heading into the studio to meet up with his brothers.

He'd been running a little late, and of course, had hit every red light on the way there.

"Have you heard from Blaze?" Scott, the eldest band member asked about their resident bad-boy.

"Not since last night, why?"

"Nothing." Scott shook his head, like he was clearing a thought. "Let's get started."

For the next two hours, Nick constantly looked over his shoulder, waiting for Blaze to arrive.

No sign of the tattooed man.

"'I'm gonna kill him."

Before they started filming, management pulled them all aside.

Sarah, their main agent, a tiny little thing with black hair, started yelling.

When she yelled, they all cringed.

"Can anyone tell me where Blaze is?" She turned her sharp eye on Nick. "You were the last one to see him, right?"

Nick could only nod.

"So, where the hell is he?"

He knew better than to lie to Sarah. She could tell when something was up.

Next thing he knew, Nick was telling them all what had happened, what *he* thought was going on.

"You've got five minutes. Find out where he is!"

He stepped away from the group. Before calling Blaze, he dialed Hope.

"Hey, I wondered if you'd call."

Her voice was the most comforting thing.

"Yeah, I had to be at the studio early for rehearsals. How're you holding up?"

She was silent for a moment. "Honestly, not good. I can't get ahold of Grace; it keeps going to voicemail. That's not like her."

"Babe," he began, but should he share?

"What's going on, Nick? There's something you're not telling me."

How does she know?

"Blaze didn't show up for rehearsals. We're about to tape and he's not here."

"Oh, shit."

There's more." Nick took a breath and launched into his suspicions about his brother.

"Nick! You have to do something!"

"I know. I'm gonna call Blaze as soon as I get off with you; find out where he is. I'll get on a plane and fly to Denver if I need to."

"Can you?" she asked, desperation clear in her voice. "I need you to go check on my friend. I'd fly there myself if I could."

"I know, baby. I'll keep you posted."

He let her go and promptly called Blaze.

The moment his friend answered, background noise revealed where he was.

The airport.

"What the hell, dude? You leave in the middle of the night and don't tell anyone? Did nothing I say last night sink in?"

"I'm sorry. I couldn't sleep. I had to do something." Blaze's voice was just as worried as Hope's had been.

"And you couldn't wait until after the goddamn taping to get a flight out? You left me to explain to not only management, but the boys, why you didn't bother to show up! Not fucking cool! Scott's freaking out; you know how he is, big brother and all. And what about Hope?"

"Attention guests in the terminal, we will begin..."

"Bro, I can't hear you. I'll call when I land." Blaze didn't let his friend get another word in.

Damn, it.

Nick returned to his band and Sarah, still cursing in his head. "He's at the airport, on his way to Denver."

"I hope you can pack fast. You're going after him."

Not even ten minutes later, he called Blaze again. It went straight to voicemail. "You're probably in the air but I wanted to let you know, as soon as we finish on Jimmy I'm heading to the airport. Already have a car lined up. I just need you to text me the address. Bro, it's not for you. I mean, it is. But I promised Hope I'd do everything I could."

HE SIGHED. The rental car employee handed him the keys to a Honda Civic.

Not the car his manager had secured for him, but at this point, Nick didn't care.

If someone had given him a Honda Civic just a week or two ago, he would've thrown a mini tantrum, pulled the *'but I'm famous'* card, and gotten what he wanted.

Today, he felt like a different man, because of Hope.

It was almost six p.m., and Blaze should get into town any moment, too.

They were both worried about what they were going to walk into.

He's been acting weird, I really hope he hasn't started using again.

His brother had been clean for almost a year now.

Drugs made people unstable and do things they otherwise wouldn't. So yeah, Nick was scared for Grace; he was scared for his brother, and he was scared for his best friend.

While he waited for them to bring his rental car around, he grabbed his phone to call Blaze.

It took a few rings before his friend answered.

"I've landed, obviously, and I'm waiting for my rental. What's your ETA and where am I going?" he asked.

"I'm in a cab; we just left the airport. Damn, I wish I'd known when you were landing. We should get there about the same time, if you can drive faster than this dipshit is. Thank God. I need you there, because I don't know what I'll do to Charles if he's hurt her," Blaze said.

"I know. I'm right there with you. I don't know what'll happen next. But I'm sure Grace is okay. She seems like a strong woman. Charles… has been acting weird, the lashing out." Nick's voice wavered, revealing some of that fear. "I gotta let you go; I need to set up my GPS. I'll see you there."

"Thanks, Nick."

"Dude, don't go in without me. Promise."

It wouldn't end well if Blaze went in alone.

"Then you better fly like the wind."

CHAPTER 14

Hope had never had a harder time concentrating than she did that day.

She'd fed the dogs twice—not that they minded.

They kept slipping between her feet as she moved around the house.

"Damn it, Moose, you're gonna kill me if you don't stop that," she screamed at the little yorkie when he almost tripped her for the third time. "I'm going outside. You," she pointed at the three small dogs that followed her. "You will stay here."

She tended the horse, mucking her stall and cleaning out her water trough.

Hope did everything she could to keep herself busy. She tried not to think about Nick, who'd called her on his way to the airport.

It would be hours before she heard from him again.

There'd still been no word from Grace.

Hope made inquiries with neighbors and her co-workers. If she needed to leave, there would be very little notice. She'd need to have things figured out beforehand.

After doing the dishes and a few loads of laundry, she packed an overnight bag with the essentials.

Just in case.

Around six p.m., Nick called.

"Baby. Pack a bag. You're flying to Denver tomorrow."

"What? Why?" Hope heard the waver in his voice. Why was he having issues getting words out?

"It's Grace. She's in the hospital. She's alive, but she needs you. Needs us all."

"Nick? What the hell happened?"

"Are you sitting down?"

"No." Hope's hands were shaking.

"I need you to sit, then I'll tell you."

"Okay. I'm ready." She really wasn't.

How could she prepare to hear why her best friend was in the hospital?

"It was Charles. He kidnapped her in her own home. Hope, he hurt her." Nick sniffled. He was actually crying.

"He broke her wrist; I know for sure. When Blaze and I got there, she was… she had…" he could barely speak.

Her eyes filled with tears, and she swallowed. "I don't want to know. Just tell me she's gonna be okay. And Charles is in jail."

"My brother," he emphasized, "is in surgery. Grace stabbed him in the leg with a knife."

"Good!" Her anger surged and she couldn't hold it back.

"Your flight's at 3:12 p.m. It's the only flight I could get you on. It goes to Seattle with a layover, then gets into Denver at 10:42 pm. I'm sorry. I wish I could get you here faster. You should have the email anytime now." There was a change in Nick's voice. He went from intense caring, to distant.

Why? Because I think Charles should be in jail? What the hell?

She could only guess. "Thank you," Hope whispered.

"I gotta go. I need to call my sister and let her know. Call me tomorrow, before you get on the plane."

She sat on the couch, staring at her phone. She had more questions than answers but couldn't handle the knowledge.

It was going to be another sleepless night.

THE PASCO AIRPORT was small and security only took a few minutes, but Hope was still there almost an hour before her flight.

She didn't check a bag; she just had her carry-on suitcase.

She ordered a coffee at the small cafe stand and sat at her gate.

Hope pulled a small travel-sized bottle from her bag and poured half of the contents into her coffee.

"Is your coffee too hot?" an older gentleman sitting next to her, asked.

"Oh, it's coconut rum."

"You scared to fly?" the man continued to push.

"No. I don't mind flying. I have anxiety until the plane gets off the ground. But this," she shook the bottle, "isn't for that."

"I see." He arched a bushy eyebrow, obviously confused.

It wasn't anxiety that was causing Hope to have alcohol at two in the afternoon. It was a different fear.

She was afraid for Grace since she still didn't know what her best friend was going through.

She was worried about Nick.

He hadn't called her all day and after their last conversation, and things had gotten tense.

Hope could only imagine what Nick was going through.

His baby brother had done something horrible.

She didn't have all the details, but it didn't sound good. Surely Charles would go to jail after he healed from whatever injury he had.

She just wanted to get to Grace. She pulled her phone out of her purse and sent Nick a text.

. . .

HOPE: I'm at the airport, at my gate.

A REPLY CAME INSTANTLY. *NICK: Okay. let me know when you get to Seattle.*

SHE'D BEEN HOPING for more. More texting, or better yet, a phone call.

She needed him as much as Grace needed her. Hope needed to be strong for her best friend. How?

Grace had always been the rock in their friendship. No matter, she'd figure it out. Hope would be strong for her friend.

The flight to Seattle was a quick one. Not even enough time for the attendants to pass out drinks.

When she landed and got to her next gate, she texted Nick again.

HOPE: At my gate in Seattle. Any update?

NICK: One step closer, but many miles farther apart. Glad you'll be here soon. Psychiatrist came to evaluate Chuck. Waiting on results. Grace's doing good. Blaze is getting things set up to move her to L.A...

HOPE: Okay. Boarding.

NICK: K, see you soon.

. . .

Hope wanted to rest, but her mind was all over the place. She had a three-hour flight ahead of her. She tried playing Nick's solo album through her headphones, but instead of soothing her, it got her agitated.

She switched to her new *Razor's Edge* playlist and tried to focus on the lyrics of the songs. She found one that really hit home. She needed to hear the words.

I'm here, my love
You were perplexed in the beginning
My dear, wipe the wet from your eyes
You'd lost your faith, it told me
There could be no more deceit
Standing there, in mystery
Holding on, could you want me
I'll do it now, what do you need
I will help so that you can succeed

I'm here, my love. I'm here, my love
I can take away all of your pain
I'll never leave, I'll never leave
You will always have me by your side
I'm here, my love. I know you
Your days will be filled with our light
Since I'm not afraid
I'll show you, That everything will be all right

Hope played the song over and over until she'd memorized the words. It made the time move along faster. She was just starting to relax when the captain announced their descent.

Her heart thundered. She was so close. Close to a man she feared she was falling in love with. Close to seeing her best friend, who may or may not be the same woman she was five days before.

Close to realizing her life had changed forever.

She grabbed her purse from under her seat and her duffle bag from the overhead, then took a deep breath as she stepped off the plane.

Nick was waiting for her just outside the security check.

She'd thought she'd held herself together well enough until Hope stepped into his open arms. The flood of tears took over.

She couldn't stop crying. It didn't matter she was in an airport full of people pushing past them.

He held her like nothing was wrong. After a moment, Nick kissed the top of her head. "Come on, baby. Let's get outta here. My hotel's right across the street from the hospital. I'm in a Marriott that has a full kitchen in the rooms. I'll make you something to eat, you can have a hot shower. We'll go see Grace in the morning."

"Thank you," was all she could get out.

HOPE SAT at the kitchen table, sipping a cup of coffee.

Nick had been amazing the night before. He'd cooked a delicious meal, ran a hot bath, and held her until she drifted off to sleep.

She'd awoken to the smell of fresh coffee and bacon.

The shower was running, and part of her wanted to join him. Another part warned her to stay away.

Something in the way his voice had changed when she mentioned Charles going to jail had her worried.

Would their budding relationship survive something like this?

He'd said he loved her, after all.

Hope gnawed on her bottom lip. He hadn't said it again, in any texts or their short phone conversations.

Nick stepped out of the bathroom, with a small towel wrapped around his slender hips. Droplets of water escaped the strands of his hair to roll down his chest.

Look away, Hope, look away.

As if to make a point she couldn't yet understand, he dropped his towel at the door and walked to the dresser naked.

He threw her a smile. "I ordered Grace flowers; they should get delivered here soon."

"Crap! I wish I'd known. I would have warned you; she hates flowers. Especially roses."

He cringed, covered it fast. However, his shoulders caved a little. "Yeah, Blaze told me about Charles' roses."

"What?" She moved closer while he slipped on jeans. "Charles' roses?"

"Oh, yeah. You don't know about that. I guess he started leaving her roses, like a weird calling card. Blaze said no roses. So I got something else."

An hour later, they stood outside Grace's door.

"Hold these and let me go in first. She doesn't know you're here." Nick handed her the enormous bouquet of daisies, and hurried into the room.

Hope dared peek inside.

Her man proceeded to the side of her bestie's bed with caution.

Grace reached for him with her right hand; her left was in a sling.

"I'm so sorry," he said.

"You have nothing to be sorry for."

"But I do. If only I'd been a better brother; if only I hadn't antagonized him. I should've known from the first night I met you at the ball; he was obsessed with you. We could have prevented all this."

"Nick, we both know this would've happened, no matter what. None of us did anything wrong. Charles needed help. He hid that from all of us. There was no way of knowing it would come to this. But trust me, I played the *what if game* for three days. It always came back to the same thing. Only Charles is to blame here. I hope this gets him the help he so desperately needs."

"Oh, I have something for you."

Her friend cocked her head to the side.

Nick put his index finger up, then left the room.

Hope stepped back before either of them saw her.

"Babe, stay right behind me. I'm gonna hold the flowers up so she can't see you..."

They got right up to the bed.

Hope stepped around Nick and into Grace's view. "Hi, Elvis." She wiped at the tears pouring down her cheeks.

"Hope! You know, I really hate that nickname!"

She threw her arms around her bestie. Hope released her and took a tentative step backward. "Oh! I'm so..."

"Do not say *sorry*! I can't hear another person say sorry!"

Her mouth dropped open.

Grace's harshness took her aback.

"It's just... this was no one's fault. Don't be sorry. I'm just glad you're here," Grace said, and her voice was a tad softer.

"I wish I could've gotten here sooner."

"You're here now, that's all that matters."

Nick stepped up behind Hope and wrapped his arms around her protectively. "We're both here for you if you need anything. I hope you know that."

Did she know that? Was he really gonna be there?

Could Hope handle it if he wasn't?

CHAPTER 15

Hope spent the entire day with Grace, getting all the details of her trauma. She cringed at her best friend's explanation of the horrors she'd endured at the hands of a man she'd thought was a dear friend.

She couldn't imagine how Grace would move forward after something like that. But her friend was strong. It'd take time and support, but she'd get through it.

Nick and Blaze had made themselves scarce, giving them much-needed girl time.

It gave Hope a chance to talk about what'd been stalking her brain. Nick.

"I mean, he wasn't rude or anything. Just a little standoffish. He hasn't brought his brother up since then. But he also hasn't been, well… the same."

Her bestie grabbed her hand. "Don't worry too much. This is traumatic for him, too. He takes some of the blame on himself, thinking he wasn't a good enough brother. You need to be there for him, as much as for me. Maybe more. I saw the look on his face when he held you when you first got here. He looked like a man in love. But only *he* could say for sure."

"I still can't believe he said he loved me on national TV! I expected it from Blaze, but not Nick."

"Yeah, I was as surprised as you were. On both counts. I have no doubt of Blaze's love for me. But how do you feel about Nick's declaration?"

"I don't know," Hope said honestly. "I mean, what girl doesn't want a hot, famous man to announce to the world they are loved? But…"

"You think it was for show?" Grace said the words she was afraid to voice

Hope could only nod.

"I hate to ask this because I am so grateful, but how long are you here for?"

"You know, I have no idea. I just packed a bag and left. My ticket was only one way. I wish I could stay as long as you need me, but…"

"You have a life in Washington. Animals that need you, a job to get to. I know. I appreciate you coming. Even if it's only for a day or two. It means a lot to me."

"I'm sorry, Miss," a nurse called from the door. "I'm afraid visiting hours are over."

Hope gave her bestie another big hug. She wasn't quite ready to let her go. She held back tears, trying to be strong.

Grace had a lot of healing to do. Most of that was emotional.

"I'll come to see you first thing in the morning if that's okay," she said.

Her friend wiped at a tear that slipped from Hope's eye. "They're releasing me in the morning. I'm not sure what's gonna happen next. I can't go back to my apartment. Ever. Besides, Blaze insisted on having professional movers finish up what I'd started. As far as I know, all my stuff is already on its way to L.A.. I'll have Blaze bring me to Nick's room after they discharge me. We can all sit and chat and figure out where we go from here."

With great reluctance, Hope left Grace's room. She sent Nick a text while walking back to the hotel, across the street.

HOPE: Leaving Grace, they kicked me out. Heading to the room. Hope you're okay.

NICK: Blaze and I are just tying up a few loose ends. See you soon.

HOPE: Any thoughts on dinner? Do you have things in the fridge I could make something?

NICK: Whatever is fine.

His 'WHATEVER' had her worried. She could take it so many different ways. Hope tried to push past the worst of them.

He's had trauma, too. Remember that.

She rummaged the fridge when she got to the room, glad the hotel he'd chosen had a full kitchen.

She'd stayed in one like it, years ago. Hadn't needed the kitchen then; it was the only hotel in the area.

Hope was pleasantly surprised by her options. For someone that didn't know how long he'd be there, Nick had clearly meal-prepped. Everything went with something.

There was enough food to make at least four different dinners, not to mention eggs, bacon, and bread.

She grabbed the package of spaghetti noodles and a jar of sauce out of the small cupboard. She made a large pot, in case Blaze would be joining them.

Hope was setting the small table when Nick arrived, Blaze in tow.

She pulled another plate and fork from the cupboard. "I hope you're hungry," she told them when the door closed.

"Starving. Thank you, Hope. You didn't have to do that," the dark-haired man said. Blaze sat at the table and opened one of the beers he was carrying.

"I picked you up a bottle of Moscato while we were out. It's not cold, but would you like a glass?" Nick held up the wine to show her.

"Yes, please. I could really use some, after today." She dished out the meal.

Nick got her wine poured. Then, he too, cracked open a beer.

"Rough day, Hope?" Blaze asked.

"It was hard hearing what happened. Grace talked about it like it was a play she was in, rather than something that happened *to* her. It's worrying me."

"Agreed," Blaze said. "That's why she's moving in with me."

"Excuse me?"

Had she heard him right?

"Well, it just makes sense. I have a four-bedroom home, and a housekeeper that comes twice a week. My place is close to the theater, and she won't be alone at night. That's what I worry about most."

"I understand that, Blaze. But you two just met. Literally."

"I know. Two weeks ago today. And your point?"

Her hackles were up. This was her best friend they were talking about. "My point is, you don't really know each other! And add a major trauma on top of that! Don't you ever watch movies? Relationships that start with a disaster, end with one! Grace can't handle that."

He took a long pull of his beer, his dark eyes burrowing into her. "You of all people should understand. When love hits you, it doesn't need an explanation, a timestamp, or anyone's approval."

"What do you mean, *me* of all people?"

Blaze glanced at his buddy.

Nick was quietly eating his meal, keeping to himself.

"Nevermind." Blaze shook his head. "I guess, I just mean, I care about her. No... I *love* her. I can say that with absolute certainty. I will do anything, *be* anything she needs. And you can bust my balls if I don't."

Hope needed Nick to break his silence. She glared. "And how do you feel about this?"

"I don't know. I can see from both sides, and either option is good. I think she should still move into the place her boss set up for her, and Blaze, you can stay with her for a while. Give her a chance to stand on her own two feet first. If you still feel you need to live together, give *her* the chance to make that decision."

"Yeah, okay. I guess you're right," Blaze said.

Hope huffed.

Really, he gives into Nick that easily?

Grace is gonna have her hands full with this one.

They finished their meal without another word about Grace.

Her bestie's man finally left around midnight, after the six-pack of beer was gone. Apparently, he was right down the hall.

This *was* the only hotel close to the hospital.

Hope had been looking forward to some much-needed alone time with Nick, but by the time his buddy left, they were both too tired to do much more than brush their teeth and crawl into bed.

It surprised her when Nick pulled her body against his, and they fell asleep curled up together.

RAYS of early morning light filled the room.

Hope dared a glance at her bedmate. She met his dark blue eyes and read in them what *she* was feeling.

Without words, she reached for him.

Her kiss was desperate as she tugged his shirt off.

Nick complied, showing he wanted her just as much.

She pressed him down on his back, kissing him as she slipped a hand under the waistband of his boxers. Her fingers curled around his hard shaft, and she reveled in the soft skin on the tip. There was the tiniest drop of moisture and she used it to her advantage. Hope stroked him softy, and smiled when he let out the smallest moan. Her lips found his again, and she stole the sound away. She broke their kiss to pull off his boxers.

"Hope, are you sure?"

She met his eyes, her heart full of fear of being rejected.

Nick hadn't touched her since L.A. Did he still want her, or was she just there for moral support?

"It's just that you've had a trying couple of days, I don't want to wear you out."

His reply was not what she expected.

"I need you, Nick, right now."

She didn't care that they didn't have condoms. She'd thought about it in the past, and had decided since she was on birth control and they hadn't used one before, why bother now?

Nick pulled her against him, laying them back down, with her stretched on top of him. His hands roamed her body.

She still wore pajamas.

Hope moved her lips to his neck, then up to his ear.

He groaned in pleasure as her tongue explored.

She pushed to her knees and took off her shirt before resuming kissing her way down his sculpted body, her full breasts gliding against him.

Nick tensed, then sucked in a breath when she kissed his hip bone.

She adjusted herself on the bed.

She'd been wanting to do this for so long.

Hope ran her tongue from the base of his cock to the tip.

He groaned, and his fingers tightened on her shoulder. It was the only part of her he could reach.

She swirled her tongue around his tip before wrapping her lips around him.

The noise he made had her smiling to herself.

She loved giving him pleasure. Hope worked him up and down until he was practically writhing, then she hummed.

Nick gripped the sheets on either side of them. "Oh, Hope," he grunted.

She worked him to the brink, tasting the little of him he could no longer hold back. Hope quickly slipped off her shorts and panties and straddled him.

At first, she just ground against him, letting the moisture between them build, then she settled into place and plunged herself down on him.

They both gasped at the pleasure of being together again.

She rode him, squeezing him with her thighs. Spending hours in the saddle on a horse had done her good.

Nick bucked beneath her, but kept her rhythm.

They took their time, the ecstasy building in both of them.

Just when Hope couldn't breathe anymore, her body exploded in spasms around him.

He released himself into her.

Hope collapsed on top of him, completely spent.

This time, their love making meant so much more... She couldn't put it to words, but maybe she loved him?

Nick gently rubbed circles on her back as they both caught their breath. "So I'm guessing you missed me?" He smirked.

They made eye contact and she arched an eyebrow. "Now, what made you think that?"

He smiled and kissed her again. "I missed you too, baby."

CHAPTER 16

"Since you showed me all the sights in L.A., I wanna show you Denver, and all the things that were important to me, growing up here." Hope slipped on a pair of jeans and a T-shirt, while Nick finished cleaning up from breakfast.

"That sounds intriguing."

"I should warn you, it's the things I found important, not what tourists think matter. Just so you know." She slipped on her shoes.

"Am I driving, or are you?"

Hope flashed a devilish grin, and he dropped the keys to his rented Honda into her capable hands.

They jumped in the car and headed north.

"Damn, babe. Are we driving to Canada?" Nick teased after twenty minutes on the road.

"This is Denver, Nick. It takes half an hour to go ten blocks. But look to your right, that's *the Grizzly Rose*. Grace and I used to go line-dancing there on Sunday nights, before I was twenty-one. Our other favorite place, *Cactus Moon*, was torn down a few years after I became of age."

"Really? You used to line-dance?"

Hope laughed. "Used to? Oh, honey. I still do. And it would make you hard to watch me move." Her cheeks burned as soon as she closed her lips.

Had she really just said that?

"You'll show me?"

"Someday. Not today. I have too many other things to show you."

They sped along I-25 toward her former part of town.

Hope kept watching his face, as he took in all the sights. She pointed to things as they passed by. "Over there is *Water World*, it's our water park. It was pretty cool when I was a kid. No idea what it looks like now. And here, on the right, that *Walmart*, it used to be a huge shopping center, where *Cactus Moon* was."

He nodded and smiled, as she reminisced about the days gone.

They finally turned off the highway, and Hope took a right turn. After two lights and a few more turns, she pulled into the parking lot of a community center.

"Where are we?" Nick asked, wearing a mix of curiosity and confusion.

"This is the *NorthDen Community Center*. Inside there's a small theater that holds about 150 people. It's where Grace and I met."

Without waiting for her to turn the engine off in the car, Nick jumped out and headed for the main entrance. He walked with a bit of swagger.

She could sit there and enjoy the view, but she was learning, not to leave him to his own devices.

Hope had just caught up with him, as he spoke with the lady at the front desk, who was eight shades of red.

"I'm sorry, I really wish I could let you in, but..." She looked down at something in front of her, as if unable to keep her eyes on Nick. "They're taking all the seats out right now. We are about to tear the place down."

"Tear it down? Why?" Hope blinked. There was the tale-tell burning of tears in her eyes.

"They're building a new rec center. This one is just so outdated."

Nick leaned closer to the woman. "All the more reason to let me in. I need to see the stage that helped launch a star."

She poked him in the side. Sure, she wanted to see the place again, but not at the cost of him lying.

"What?" he asked, sparing her a glance.

"I'm not a star."

"Not yet. But you could be." Nick turned back to the lady. "Just a peek? Is there a side door we could go through? It doesn't have to be the main entrance."

The woman picked up a small sign that read, "be right back" in bold letters, and set it on the counter. "All right. But we need to be quick."

He grabbed Hope's hand, and they followed.

It brought her back in time, to a place that'd given her confidence when she didn't know she'd needed it. Also, a friend she'd do anything for.

It'd been far too many years since she'd seen the small theater, but the memories came rushing back.

They took the stairs that lead to the dressing rooms below the stage.

It looked so different, yet so much the same.

Hope went straight to the countertop where she and Grace had shared their bags of *Reese's Pieces* while getting ready.

She looked under the counter, and there, carved into the wood where no one would see, was their initials, along with "BFF."

Best friends forever.

"What're you looking at," Nick asked, leaning down beside her.

"The mark we left. But it, too, will be gone soon." She straightened, and couldn't help the tears from falling. "I didn't realize what this place meant to me until now. I can't believe it's going away."

He held her, kissing the top of her head. "The building may be going, but your memories never will be. You didn't even know it was being torn down until just now. Had she not told you, would you still be crying?"

"Probably."

The employee took them on to the stage and let them stand in the middle. She kept a close eye to make sure they didn't go where they shouldn't, since there was a construction crew slowly demolishing the space.

Hope watched as they carefully worked to remove the old theater seats. "Are they saving the seats for something?" she asked.

"Oh, yes! Everything that can be salvaged is going to a new theater in downtown for underprivileged kids!"

Her heart lifted. At least they weren't going to the city dump. That would've been more than she could bear.

Nick wrapped an arm around her waist and kissed the top of her head again. "I know you have some pretty amazing memories of this place. And I don't want the sadness you are feeling, seeing it coming apart, be what you hold on to. So…" He took a step back, holding her hands, took a deep breath, then sang.

Honey, beg for your forgiveness
Don't leave, you're the light in here
Touch me here, I need you
The late hour is making me tired
Baby, Can you make me the man that you need, my love

My past, it cannot be undone

Pretending to be what I'm not
Actor I was, Left you unaware
So let me display the Designs of Love

HE FINISHED, and the rec center employee squealed.

"Oh! *Designs of Love*! That's my favorite *Razor's Edge* song! How did you know?"

Hope looked into Nick's blue eyes and they both let out a quiet laugh.

He turned to look at the other woman, putting on all his charm. "It's my way of saying thank you. It means a lot to me that you let us in here. We'll get outta your hair now."

They retreated to the safety of the red Honda and burst into full laughter.

"I thought that lady was gonna pass out. Does that happen to you often?" She started the car.

"More than I'd like to admit. I just hope she doesn't share what happened for a day or two. Let me get outta town and back to L.A. before the fans start hunting for me in Denver."

Instead of finding humor in his comment, it tore at Hope's heart.

Was he looking forward to getting back to his normal life and away from her?

She didn't know when she'd see him again.

She pushed her depressing thought to the back of her head, reminding herself to live in the moment.

As short-lived as it might be.

"WHAT THE HELL IS THIS PLACE?" Nick asked when his girl pulled into the only empty parking spot in a full lot.

He looked around the shopping complex. It looked like any other cheap shopping center, with a daycare, dollar store, and smoke shop.

However, there was a huge, pink, Spanish-inspired building that had him confused.

"It's *Casa Bonita*," Hope said, pure glee twinkling in her hazel eyes.

"Yeah, I can see the name. But what is it?"

"It's a restaurant. And a dive show. And so much more."

He laughed. "Like in the *South Park* episode?"

"The what?" She frowned.

They headed toward the entrance. "I should've guessed. You're not a *South Park* fan?"

She shook her head, and her cheeks flushed pink.

"Yeah. Didn't think so." Nick took her hand and let him lead the way.

Inside, they had to go down a corridor to reach the hostess. She took their orders, 'all-you-can-eat platters', and sent them on.

"You mean we carry our own food?" He blinked. He'd never carried his own food to his table at a restaurant. Not to mention, the food didn't look very appetizing, either.

"Yup. And when we get to the top of the ramp, that's where they decide where to seat you. We want to ask to be as close to the waterfall as possible."

Nick looked around. The place was *just* like the cartoon show. There was a *mariachi* band playing, and a huge waterfall.

The place looked like it had to be the biggest restaurant he'd ever been into.

The attendant took them to a table, right next to the waterfall, like they'd asked.

Their waitress joined them soon and explained the use of the red flag, to raise it anytime they needed something.

For a Monday night, the place was rather busy.

Seemingly unashamed of her appetite, Hope devoured her

chicken all-you-can-eat meal. She even went back for a second round of cheese enchiladas. "I know most people don't like the food here, but I'm the exception. I love the chicken."

Nick picked at his beef enchilada. It tasted about as good as it looked. But he'd been all around the world and had eaten cuisine in every country.

What did he expect from some weird, off-the-wall restaurant in the outskirts of Denver?

The sopapillas, on the other hand, were delicious. He raised the flag three times for more, even though it wasn't healthy.

Nick had been eating a very low-carb diet for the past few years. He could have a treat once in a while, and he'd work it all off when he got back to L.A..

He had six weeks of rehearsals ahead of him. Not to mention, a nine-month tour. A few sopapillas wouldn't hurt.

After they finished their meal, his petite beauty showed him around the restaurant.

There were caverns, a palace themed room, a veranda room, and a theater. Even a cave that reminded him of a cheesy funhouse.

Nick's favorite thing about the night was the old fashion photo studio. They picked out some slip-on garments that made them look like a gunslinger and a saloon girl, and posed in front of a backdrop.

In all his years of *Razor's Edge* and being on the road, he'd never done something like that.

It was ridiculous, and yet the funnest thing he'd done in a long time.

Besides having Hope naked beneath him, of course.

It was close to ten p.m. before they finally made their way back to the hotel.

He'd thoroughly enjoyed the day, and getting to glimpse Hope's past. It made him feel a bit closer to her.

Hope's driving gave him time to contemplate what Blaze had

said about being in love after two weeks. It was clear the depth of their love, his buddy and Grace.

He felt the same way about Hope. He knew he loved her.

Does she love me, too?

She hasn't said as much yet.

There was still so much more he needed to know about her. *Wanted* to know. And the four letter word he needed from her was at the top of his mind.

The time would come when Nick could say he knew everything about her. That time wasn't now.

He wasn't looking forward to telling her he had to head back in the morning.

CHAPTER 17

They were barely out of the car when the bright lights of cellphone flashes and video cameras blinded them.

Nick rushed around to Hope's side, pulling her as close to his body as he could.

All the while the paparazzi bombarded them with questions.

"Nick, it is true your brother is being booked on assault charges?"

"Hey, where's Blaze? Heard he was locked up with some broad."

"Nick, who's the new trollop?"

"Is it true the upcoming joint tour is being canceled because of your family drama?"

Normally, he'd take the time to answer a few questions, while continuing to walk to wherever his destination was.

This time, he needed to hurry away from them.

Hope tensed beside him, shrinking into his space.

"No comment tonight. Thank you." Nick pushed past the last few and into the hotel lobby.

Unfortunately, one man followed. He must've thought he was

being sneaky, keeping his cellphone down, but the camera was clearly pointed in their direction.

This wasn't Nick's first time dealing with a guy like this.

He pressed the second floor's button, not their floor, then waited.

The other man didn't choose a floor.

Hope wore a quizzical expression that her creased eyebrows.

He couldn't say anything, only nodded to acknowledge her confusion.

The doors opened.

"Have a nice night," Nick said to the man, a bit forcefully. He grabbed Hope's hand and rushed her out.

Without a word, he headed down the hallway, toward the door to the stairwell. He stopped at a room, just a few doors from the stairs, and pretended to look for his room key, which was tucked away in his wallet.

He needed time to make sure the man wasn't following them.

Luckily, the paparazzi had continued on in the elevator.

Nick bolted for the stairwell, leading Hope to take the steps up to the last level.

They were alone.

He pulled the key out and rushed her into their room.

The moment the door was closed, Hope burst into tears.

Nick wrapped his arms around her and let her soak his shirt with her tears. Sure, he had sisters and had dealt with tears before, but this… What was he supposed to do?

She didn't have a reason to cry.

At least, not any reasons he could think of.

They'd had a marvelous day, visiting pieces of her life.

What could she possibly be crying about?

Should he ask?

He held on tight, but walked her further into the room, trying to get to the box of tissues on the desk.

When he could finally reach one, he stuck it between them.

It took her a moment to realize it was there and she peeled herself off him.

Nick wanted to hold her out by her shoulders and ask "what the hell is wrong with you?" but she spoke before he could form the words.

"How do you live like that?"

What?

"I'm sorry," he sputtered.

"People, in your face like that! Does it happen often?" She wiped at her tears.

"Um, yeah. Most days. You just get used to it."

Hope pushed away from him. "No."

He waited a moment, frowning. He cocked his head to one side. "No? No, what?"

"No, I won't get used to it. This didn't happen in L.A.. If I'd known…"

"Damn it, Hope. What're you saying?" Nick went to the fridge and pulled out a beer. He didn't drink often, and he'd had a margarita with dinner. However, her drastic shift was getting to him.

"Nothing." She let out a huff and retreated to the bathroom, locking the door behind her.

Nick took a long pull on the beer.

What the fuck was that about?

He pulled his phone out and called Blaze. "Hey, how is Grace holding up?"

"As well as can be expected. I think she's looking forward to heading to L.A. tomorrow and starting new. She needs to put all this behind her. I'm glad management got on board and hooked us up with the company plane. I don't think she could handle all the stares on a commercial flight. My beautiful woman does have a few visible marks. She's brave. And stronger than most people I know. But she's been through a lot."

"Yeah, she has. And at the hands of my little brother. I don't know if I can look her in the eye and not be overwhelmed with grief. Surely, there could've been somethi–"

"Don't go there, bro. You'll tear yourself apart with the 'what-ifs'. You've always been a great brother. Chuck just has issues. He always has. But never like this. No one could have seen this coming," Blaze said.

His best friend was right. Speaking of best friends, it wasn't the right time to ask for help with Hope. He'd have to figure her out on his own.

Wasn't that what Nick had been thinking just hours ago?

Getting to know her, *all* of her.

That meant the bad, too.

"What time is the flight?" he asked, needing a subject change.

"Takeoff is at 2:30 p.m. So, I suggest we head to the airport around noon. What about Hope? Is she flying with us to L.A.? Or commercial back to… where does she live?"

"Washington," Nick heard Grace say in the background.

"I…uh…don't know. I'll talk to her after she gets out of the bathroom. Guess I'm driving everyone to the airport tomorrow?"

"You're the only one with a car, so please. Wanna meet for breakfast first?"

Blaze, always the smart one.

Not.

"Yeah, I'm sure Hope will want to see Grace one more time, just in case."

They finalized their plans and said their goodbye's.

Nick finished his beer and waited for Hope to get out of the bathroom.

After a while, he started getting irritated.

What is taking her so long?

He got another beer.

He'd heard the water turn on, and assumed she was taking a bath.

She really liked baths.

Nick really liked joining her in them.

He tried the door, but as suspected, it was locked.

He'd had enough.

"Hope, what's going on in there?"

She didn't reply.

Nick knocked harder. "Babe. can you open the door?"

Nothing.

"God damn it, what the fuck is going on?"

There was no reason for her to ignore him.

He continued his rant at the closed door. "I don't understand you. We had a great day. Then you break down into tears and storm off. I can't get to know you better when you block me like this. Talk to me!"

Nothing.

That was it.

Growing up with siblings that did things like this, he'd learned how to pick a lock.

Nick rushed to the desk and found his target. A paperclip in the information packet from the hotel.

He twisted the small metal into a mostly straight line. The bathroom door had a tiny hole where he slipped the clip in.

After a little wiggling, he heard the telltale sound of the lock clicking.

"What the fuck is going on, Hope?" he practically screamed at her.

She was lying in the bathtub, the water murky from soap, and hiding most of her body.

Hope didn't move, despite his yell.

His heart thundered in his ears, and bile was creeping up to choke him. "Hope?" He reached for her; moving at what seemed like slow motion, to touch her.

Her skin was warm.

Okay, she's alive.

His hand on her shot her straight up; water splashed everywhere.

"Shit!" Hope squealed, pulling white headphones from her ears.

He hadn't seen them when he'd come in.

She looked around, her eyes finally landing on him. "I guess I fell asleep."

He didn't move, as residual shock still swirled in his gut.

"Can you hand me a towel? This water's freezing," she said.

She has no clue I was yelling at her.

He grabbed the closest towel and passed it her way.

"Nick? Are you okay? You look like you've seen a ghost."

He swallowed once, then twice, before he could finally find his voice. "I was calling for you and you weren't answering. I thought you…" he couldn't say the words.

His sister's death dominated his brain. He hadn't been there, hadn't seen her, but had visualized, more than once, what it would've looked like.

Hope wasn't suicidal, but the thought of his sister still lingered.

"I'm sorry. I had my earbuds in. I can't believe I fell asleep. Guess I was more tired than I realized." She started drying her hair, obviously still having no idea what she'd done to him.

Rather than start a fight, Nick turned on his heels and stepped back into the bedroom. He paced for a few moments, trying to get his thoughts back in line.

Do I just drop it, or push, and find out why she was crying?

He assumed this would be their last night together for a while, and he didn't want to make it worse. How could he be there for her in the future, if he didn't know what was up in the present?

I'll wait and see if she says anything. Otherwise, we can talk about it in the morning.

A yawn escaped his lips.

"See, you're tired, too," Hope teased, retreating from the now-dark bathroom. "As much as I'd love to spend tonight with you buried deep in me, I think we both need to sleep. But tomorrow night…" She twirled her finger over the bed.

Nick didn't respond while he undressed. He sighed. "I've got to go back to L.A. tomorrow. With Blaze and Grace. We've already missed the first rehearsal and will miss tomorrow, too. Management is demanding we return. Immediately."

"Oh," she whispered, climbing in beside him.

"Come with me."

"What?"

"Come with me to L.A.. I'm stuck there for the next six weeks with rehearsals. You can stay with me and help Grace during the day. It would be great!"

"Nick, you know I can't. I have a job to get back to, and animals that need me. I can't just pack up and go."

There was more to it, he could hear it in her voice. The way she'd hesitated at the end. There was something else she wanted to say, but didn't.

Hope switched the light off on her side of the bed, leaving only the faint glow from the lamp next to him. "How am I getting home?" Her voice was barely a whisper.

"I'll get you a ticket in the morning, back to Washington."

Nick flicked his light off when she rolled away from him.

CHAPTER 18

"Are you sure you can't come back to L.A.? Just for a few days?" Grace held her hand across the table at the little diner they were holed up in. Her best friend tried hard to hide the pain she was in, both physically and emotionally. It was there, in the slight crease in her brow, and the way she gently bit at her bottom lip. Two signs she was in distress.

"I wish I could. But you know how hard it was for me to get away for your show. I really do have to get back to my life. My animals need me."

Her bestie released her hand, and she watched it return to Blaze's larger one.

The man held onto Grace, like she could float away.

Hope was grateful her friend had someone now. She deserved to be loved. Truly loved.

As much as she hated to admit it, the dark-haired, tattooed, bad-boy of *Razor's Edge* was exactly what her bestie needed. Even if they'd only known each other for two weeks.

Did that matter?

It was the same time she'd known Nick.

Hope pushed those thoughts away. She didn't want to deal with any of the answers.

"What time is your flight?" Blaze asked, sounding like he was trying to help lighten the rather somber mood that seemed to surround them all.

"I got her a flight with Delta that leaves about thirty minutes before us. The agent said it was in the same terminal as our private flight. So we can stay together a little longer," Nick said.

The sadness in his voice broke her heart.

The popstar lived a life she could never be a part of.

She'd learned that last night.

It wasn't just the cameras in her face, or the paparazzi calling her a trollop. The complete invasion of privacy.

Hope was a very private person. That wasn't something she wanted to deal with.

When Nick had made her the center of attention on national television, it'd been bad enough. The games they'd played on the show were fun, and helped distract her, but the thought of being seen by millions of people had made her ill.

Was he worth it?

Unlike her best friend, who'd found instant love, that wasn't what she and Nick were experiencing...was it?

Professing one's love on TV didn't make it any more real than professing it in private.

Actually, she felt like it'd been pushed.

Was it real?

She contemplated those words over and over as they sped to the airport.

Nick was abnormally quiet; Blaze and Grace were making nauseating happy couple noises from the back seat.

She glanced down at her phone every so often, the ping of notifications drawing her back to the screen.

"You should put it on silent or turn off notifications until you get home. It'll just drive you nuts if you focus on it," Nick said, touching her hand.

"I know," she whispered.

"I promise, you really do get used to it. It's nothing but background noise. It's something Grace will learn all about in just a few hours, I'm sure." He glanced over his shoulder, trying to get his buddy's attention, yet kept his eyes on the road. "Dude. Have you given Grace the 4-1-1 on learning to be in the spotlight?"

Blaze chuckled. "Seriously, bro? She's a star in her own right. I'm sure she's been in the spotlight many times. But yeah, we had the *'talk'.*"

"Think we'll be okay at the airport?" Grace asked.

"Yeah, according to Twitter, they're all still hovering around the hospital. Guess someone told them Blaze's new toy was still there," Hope teased, trying to lighten her own melancholy mood.

"Is that why your phone's going crazy?" her bestie inquired.

"I made the mistake of going on twitter this morning, while Nick was in the shower. I wanted to see what horrible things they'd said about me last night. It's a rabbit hole I should've stayed away from."

"I told you!" he scolded. "They're full of shit."

"But they're right. Why would a guy as hot as you want a fat cow like me?" Hope's voice dropped so low; maybe they hadn't heard. Did she want them to?

"Dishonor on you, dishonor on your cow!" Grace retorted, laughter in her tone.

"Damn it, Gracie! Now's not the time for your stupid movie quotes!" Tears burned the corners of her eyes.

"Now's the *perfect* time for stupid movie quotes," Blaze said. "Never listen to the media. They want to get a rise outta you. That's how they make their money. And you're handing it to them in spades! *Hakuna Your Tatas!*"

Hope giggled, despite her dark thoughts. "I'm not sure what that means, but thanks."

"I'M NOT ready to say goodbye," Nick crooned as they stood at her gate.

The boarding had already started, but he wanted her to be one of the last on, even after she'd told him of her anxiety and desire to be one of the first people on.

"I don't even know when I'll get to see you again. It might be awhile."

She smiled. Should she comfort him or hurry away? What did Hope want?

He was an amazing man, a good brother, and a friend. Definitely the best lover she'd ever had. No one could compare to him. Not that she'd ever hold someone to that high of a standard.

It was good while it lasted.

Epic, even.

Like anything too good in life, it had to end.

He pulled her into his arms, not saying a word, and kissed her. It was a last goodbye kiss. Deep, passionate, and final.

So, he feels the same.

This really is goodbye.

Nick released her from his tight grip, sliding his hands down her arm to grab her hands. He gave a gentle squeeze and kissed her on the top of her head. "Text me when you land. I want to know you made it safe."

Hope couldn't form words, so she nodded. She slipped away from his touch and faced her best friend.

Grace gave her a hug to rival Nick's, tears streaming down her cheeks unchecked. "I'm gonna miss you! Promise you'll come to see me. Maybe Thanksgiving?" There was desperation in her long-time friend's voice.

"You know I can't make any promises, Elvis. But I'll do my best."

"That's all I ask. Now go, before I never let you leave!"

She gave her best friend one more tight hug and turned on her heels to rush for the door.

Hope couldn't look back at Nick, couldn't see his blue eyes one more time.

She was a ball of nerves her entire flight home. That wasn't abnormal. This time, she was so upset over the way things had ended; she got motion sick and had to jump up from her seat, so as not to puke on the man sitting beside her. Once again grateful she always asked for the dreaded aisle seat.

Hope wiped at the sweat on her brow, rinsed out her mouth, and returned to her seat.

The attendant had seen her distress and brought her a small glass of ginger ale to help ease her stomach.

The landing was smooth, and the moment she could turn her cell back on she sent out texts.

HOPE: Gracie, I landed. Should be home in less than an hour. How did things go for you?

HOPE: Thank you for everything, Nick. You changed my life so much in such a short time. I'll forever be grateful. I'll be home soon. Gonna crash hard.

She didn't expect an answer for a while. They were flying a further distance.

Hope was tired. Physically, mentally, emotionally. Wiped out in every way possible.

When she got home, her excited dogs greeted her. They were bouncing around. When she got inside and spotted a destroyed couch cushion, it shouted how unhappy they were with her.

The housesitter had fed all the animals that morning before

leaving, but it was late in the evening, so Hope's first order of business was to feed everyone, again.

The familiar routine relaxed her. She was home. Back to normal, back to reality.

The week she'd spend in L.A. had been a dream.

Beautiful, unreal. Perfect.

The few days she'd spent in Denver had been a bucket of ice water.

Her best friend was broken, but had an amazing man to put her back together. Grace had spent the last three years in the spotlight, so the paparazzi wouldn't be that big of a deal for her.

Just another way they were so very different.

She would miss Nick.

But it was for the better.

Hope was just crawling into bed when her phone rang.

"Hey! We landed at LAX. Blaze is gonna take me to his place tonight. We're both beat. Then tomorrow we'll go check out my new townhome. I'll call you after six, in case you go to work," Grace said.

"Thanks. I miss you all ready. But..." Tears stung her eyes. "I'm glad you have Blaze to take care of you."

How could she admit she was jealous?

Not only of the intense passion the two of them shared, but Hope was being replaced in her friend's life.

No! I can't think like that!

"You sound tired, too. Get some sleep. Love ya, sis."

"Love ya, too."

After letting her bestie go, she waited.

And waited.

An hour passed, Nick never replied.

Hope set her phone to *silent*, then placed it on her nightstand.

So I am right. We're done.

A single tear slipped down her cheek to get lost in her pillow.

If this is for the best, why does it hurt so bad?

CHAPTER 19

Nick read the text for what must've been the hundredth time. The words Hope sent didn't change.

Neither did the way he interpreted them.

"Thank you for everything, Nick. You changed my life in such a short time. I will forever be grateful."

Those were words of goodbye.

He'd dated enough women to know when they were breaking things off. It sounded just like all those times.

But hurt so much more.

He was sick to his stomach.

"Hello, Earth to Nick," Blaze said, shoulder bumping him to get his attention. "Have you listened to a word I said?"

"Uh, no. Sorry. I was just thinking."

"Are you all right? You're not looking so good," Grace said. She reached to check his forehead.

Her touch was kind, but it wasn't *her* hands he wanted on him.

"Fine. Just tired."

His best friend grabbed his upper arm and yanked to force

him his way. "Grace is right. You look like shit. Maybe you should crash at my place tonight."

Nick's cheeks flush with heat. "Nah, you two need your alone time."

Blaze chuckled and pulled his keys out of his bag. "There won't be sweet butter lovin ' tonight. She's not in any shape for that kind of activity. Sorry, babe," he turned to Grace.

Her face was molted red.

"Just leave your car here, we'll come back for it later. You need to crash," his friend finished.

"Oh, Nick. Did you call Hope?" she asked.

He shook his head. "I heard you talk to her. I know she's good. I'll try tomorrow."

Or not. Why push if she doesn't want me?

He sat on the edge of the bed in the guest room of Blaze's Burbank home. He could hear his buddy getting Grace settled in for the night.

In the morning, they'd drop him back off at the airport to get his car, before going to check out her new townhome.

Nick had to remind his buddy they still had to show up for rehearsals. Even if it was just to let everyone see they were still alive.

He also needed to get the keys to the temp apartment Sarah had secured for him. Most likely, it was in the same complex as the other guys who didn't live in L.A.. Everyone but Blaze.

Sleep eluded him.

Nick's thoughts kept returning to Hope. He turned over every thought of why she'd pushed him away.

It was subtle. But there nonetheless.

Was it something I did, or said?

Was it the paparazzi?

He'd told her he loved her, for God's sake. Did she not believe him?

Sure, living in the spotlight wasn't always easy. When a guy found someone that could be his everything, it was worth it.

Wasn't it?

Nick glanced at the clock again. *1:42 a.m.*

He just wanted to sleep!

Somewhere after two a.m., he bolted awake, after finally drifting off.

Grace was screaming.

Pure panic filled the house.

He jumped from his bed to run to the sound.

In Blaze's bedroom, his buddy was wrapped tight around Grace, holding her while she sobbed uncontrollably.

The man he called brother looked at him, and without a sound, mouthed the words, "It's okay. Go back to bed."

Nick walked like a zombie back to the guest room. A tear slipped down his cheek, leaving a hot trail.

I did this.

Why wasn't I a better brother?

No wonder Hope doesn't want me.

He let every unsavory thought fill his head and spread into his heart.

He couldn't let go of the guilt. If he'd been there for his little brother more when he grew up, rather than traversing around the globe becoming an international star, maybe Charles wouldn't have had a monster growing inside him, hidden from the world until it broke free.

Almost killing Grace.

And yet, the woman was still the kindest he'd ever met. She held no blame. None for him, and none for his brother.

She still cared about Charles.

Nick carried enough blame and guilt for them all.

At some point, he'd drifted off to sleep.

It was far from peaceful.

Nick woke feeling like he was dying. His entire body hurt. He was hot, and yet had the chills. He stumbled into the kitchen when the smell of fresh coffee drifted down the hall.

Blaze sat alone at the little cafe table in his kitchen, blowing on the hot cup of joe. "Pot's hot. Get a cup and come sit."

He followed his friend's advice, grabbing the biggest mug in the cupboard and filling it to the rim. He was hesitant about sitting, though. Nick didn't want to talk. He just wanted to drink coffee and get on with the day.

He wouldn't be that lucky.

"Dude. You okay? You really look like shit. I thought some sleep might help, but you've gotten worse. You sick?"

Thanks, Blaze.

"Maybe. I thought sleep would help, too. But I didn't get much of that." Nick cringed. He hadn't meant to insinuate it was Grace's fault. He needed to clarify. "I mean, my thoughts were everywhere and my head hurt. I just couldn't fall asleep."

"I'm sure Gracie's panic attack didn't help much," Blaze said.

"Is she gonna be okay?" He really liked the lady. She was good for his best friend, and it seemed Blaze was good for her, too.

"Yeah. It's gonna take time. The doc said she'd got PTSD. She's gonna find a therapist here to help. One day at a time. She'll probably come to rehearsals for a while, I don't think she should be alone just yet. But as we learned last night, I can't sleep next to her. Not yet. So I'm gonna stay with her in her new place. She needs to feel like she has a safe place that belongs only to her. I know she'd stay at my house, but I insist she start out there. I'll sleep on the couch until she's ready."

"Smart," Nick said in between sips of hot java.

"My point to all this; why don't you stay here? You already know where everything is, you've stayed here enough times in the past few years. No point in staying in some rundown apartment with no personality."

He laughed. Blaze's place had plenty of personality. The man hoarded antiques. The more obscure, the better. He still hadn't taken in all the odds and ends his friend had throughout the house. "Thanks, bro. I appreciate that."

"Then, I'll take you to get your car and come back to get Gracie. That'll give her a chance to have a long, hot shower, and get ready to go check out her new place. The movers should've gotten everything unpacked by now. I'm sure she will want to rearrange it all, though."

"Let me know if you need any help. Between her foot in a boot and her arm in a sling, I doubt she's gonna be able to do much more than boss you around."

Blaze chuckled. "She's not really a bossing-around type, but I get your point. Looking at you, though, I don't see you able to do much either. You should try to get some rest this afternoon. I'll go see Sarah and the guys. Take one more day to yourself."

Nick nodded, staring down into his black cup.

Two HOURS LATER, Nick's Beemer was parked in the driveway, Blaze and Grace had left, and he now stood in the shower, letting the far-too-hot water soothe his aching body.

He rarely got sick. A cold had never hit him this hard, or fast. Surely, that was all it was.

He hadn't been eating healthy the past two weeks, and had consumed far more alcohol than normal. Nick had allowed his immune system to crash, and was paying for it now.

A few days rest, lots of non-libation fluids and some healthy food, and he'd be right back on his feet.

After getting his car at the airport, he made a beeline for the grocery store.

He loaded up with all his favorites.

Nick wished he'd thought to look in Blaze's fridge before they left, so see what his buddy had in stock, but it really didn't matter.

They had different eating habits. He was usually grain-free. Something he'd given up the past fourteen days. He didn't know how long he'd be staying at his friend's house, but planned for the next two weeks.

They had six weeks of rehearsals, then they'd hit the road.

He'd downed a glass of orange juice and taken a slew of vitamins to get his system jump started. That usually helped. Nick tried to eat something, but found he had no appetite. He managed to get down some scrambled eggs he'd cooked with red peppers. It was something, at least.

He'd hoped he'd have more of a desire to eat after a hot shower.

Not so much.

Although his body needed rest, he didn't feel capable of a nap. Living on the road the past twenty years had taught him to sleep when and where he could.

Right now, his mind was in a million places, and didn't want to slow down. He wanted to text Hope and check in on her, but was afraid of rejection.

Nick needed to call on Charles and find out the status of not only his health, but the charges placed against him. Would his little brother be going to jail, or somewhere to work on his mental health?

He'd had major surgery to repair the artery in his right thigh, from where Grace had stabbed him to get away.

The doctor had said he'd had substantial muscle and tissue damage and he'd need physical therapy. When or where would that happen, considering their circumstances? He really needed to make that call.

His head hurt.

Nick sat on the brown leather sofa in Blaze's living room, flipping through channels.

Maybe I should swing by rehearsals, or at least call.

He'd left his phone in the bathroom, but didn't have the energy to go get it.

He continued to search for something to watch, something to force his mind calm. He settled on an old black and white with Humphrey Bogart. It was one he'd seen before.

Nick slipped down into the couch until he could lean his head back against the top of it. He settled into the movie, letting the life of the characters seep into him, and he drifted off to sleep.

CHAPTER 20

The next two weeks were hell for Hope. She drifted in and out of feeling ill. Not full-blown sick, but there were days when she could hardly function.

She'd tried to go back to work, but between the aches and pains, runny nose, and bouts of nausea, she'd been on the verge of tears by lunchtime each day.

To make matters worse, while trying to handle feeling like death, her young colt had stepped in a newly dug gopher hole, and broken his leg.

Hope had had no choice but to put him down. He'd been her last horse, the one that was supposed to get her back in the saddle.

She'd lost her childhood horse a few years before, and swore she'd never own another, until Buttons had come into her life.

He'd been a gift from a friend who was moving out of state and couldn't take him. She'd been hesitant in the beginning. Hadn't needed or wanted the responsibility of a new horse. However, Buttons had ended up bringing her joy she hadn't known she was missing.

With his passing, being sick, her best friend recovering from an attack, and now losing Nick, or what could've been, was sending Hope to a dark place.

"Girly, you need a new horse," her friend Krissy said.

"No, thank you," Hope said, and praying her friend couldn't see the wrinkle of her brows.

"Mazie is giving away four horses in about a month. She got loaded down with a lot that was seized from a property. They're in good health. She's being very picky about who they go to, but I think you'd be a great candidate. Please, just go check them out. If nothing else, you'll get to ride for the day."

That gave her a lift. Buttons hadn't been old enough to train for riding. It'd been years since she was on the back of a horse. It might raise her spirits. "All right. I'll go look. But only if you come with me."

The next four weeks were a blur. Hope had struggled to make it through each day.

She spoke with Grace a few times. Her friend was working through her own demons.

Grace had gone to the theater, and was finally beginning her work with the company.

Blaze was rehearsing during the day, and they were spending their evenings at her new place, making it comfortable. Not once did her friend mention Nick, other than to say they were all looking forward to going on tour.

The night before she was supposed to go to the ranch with Krissy, Hope tossed and turned, not really getting much sleep.

When the sun rose, she hopped out of bed. She tried reading for a while but couldn't concentrate. Hope was oddly excited to go see the horses. Her friend Krissy was right. A new horse would keep her very busy.

That could push her thoughts of *him* away.

After breakfast, her friend picked her up to head to the reservation. They found it with no problems. They went to the barn to get checked in.

"Good Morning," Hope said.

Someone was in a stall in the back, cleaning up. "Mornin'," the lady called back, then leaned her pitchfork against the wall and came out. She was tall and broad shouldered, with dark brown hair and eyes. She was built like a woman that grew up on a ranch. "How can I help you?" she asked, but her gaze rested on Hope.

"I called this morning about the horses," Hope said.

"Oh, yes! Krissy, is this the lady you were talking about?"

Her blonde friend nodded.

"I'm Mazie. But I'm sure Krissy already told ya. So, tell me about yourself. Why should I give a horse to you?"

"Well, I've owned horses most of my life. I had a break from having one when my childhood mare died. I had a colt until recently." She tried to hold back the tears over the loss of Buttons, but she couldn't help it.

"If you'll just come with me, I have some paperwork for ya. Then we'll get y'all saddled up."

"I'm sorry?" Hope frowned. She was only there to look at a potential horse. Sure, she'd hoped to sit in the saddle on one, feel the horse's temperament out, but paperwork? It seemed a little early for that.

"I see the concern written across your face, honey. And that's okay. Anyone that steps on my land and goes near any animal on my property signs a waiver. You won't believe how many dumbasses I have come out here, thinking they know a little something about something, and end up getting themselves hurt. Nope! Not anymore. So, let's go sign some stuff."

Mazie gave some forms, and said she was going to saddle all four horses.

Hope finished and went to help with the horses, leaving Krissy still at the table.

"How long have you been riding? I know you said you'd had a horse since childhood, but that's not the same as riding," Mazie asked, while they brushed down the horses.

"Almost 12 years now." Her attention was on the sixteen hand black gelding with a white blaze and socks the dark-haired woman had suggested she start with.

"Then you can tell me why we comb before we saddle."

Hope loved that the woman was grilling her. "We comb them with the metal curry to take the mud off and loosen the shedding hair. Always brush with the grain. Then use a rubber curry to work the dirt and loose hair off."

"Very good. Let's take these two out for a ride. Then we can come back and prepare the next two."

"What about Krissy?" she asked. Her friend had dragged her there, after all.

"She's not coming. This is between you and me. I need to see how you treat your animal when there's no one to worry about but yourself."

Once they got out into the open range, Mazie encouraged Hope to take off.

She turned her horse and walked a scant distance away from the ranch owner and her horse, before kicking up to a canter.

Her hair whipped back from her face, the warm September wind kissing her cheeks, and she was out of breath. However, she felt better than she had in a very long time.

"Did you have fun?" Mazie asked, smiling up at her from the blanket she'd set on the ground.

Her horse was secured to a tree nearby.

"Yeah, he can move," Hope said, dismounting. She led her horse to the shade and tied him next to the Mazie's mare.

They enjoyed a drink of the water the woman had packed. They talked about the history of Mazie's ranch, and how she'd ended up with the lot of seized horses.

The horse she'd rode in on was moving restlessly. He reared up, striking the air.

They both jumped up and ran to him.

The huge creature came down and was rearing up again when Hope reached him. Mazie had gone to her horse to calm him, as he was now agitated.

Hope couldn't figure out what was wrong. She kept her voice calm and reached for the rope, but the horse had pulled the slip knot too tight when he'd bucked.

When the gelding went up for a third time, she saw it.

There was a snake in the tree.

Hope grabbed the pocket knife she always kept clipped in her boot when riding, flipped it open and grabbed the reins.

As she sawed at the leather, the horse's foot struck, catching her across the left wrist.

Oh my fucking God!

The pain that burst through her wrist sent ripples up her arm and lightning filtered behind her eyes.

When she sliced through the reins, he spun and raced away.

"Are you okay?" Mazie demanded, appearing at her side.

"Yeah, I'm fine," she lied, blinking back the tears..

"He's never done that before," Mazie said, they both watched the horse disappear across the field.

"There's a snake in the tree," Hope said.

"I can't believe I didn't see that. I'm usually so much more aware of my surroundings. I'm so sorry. Come on. We can double up and head back. I'll send Tony out to get the gelding."

Hope swung up into the saddle, hooking her elbow on the saddle horn.

Once Mazie was settled, they headed back to the ranch.

Hope tried to ignore the throbbing in her wrist. She examined it subtly. No blood, that was good. She wanted to feel it, to see if it was broken, but she didn't want to draw attention to it. She'd cowgirl up and deal with it.

She didn't want anything to spoil her day. It was the first one in a while where she felt good. So she just let her hand rest lightly on the saddle horn.

By the time they'd made it back to the barn, she could feel the sweat dotting her forehead and cheeks. She was also a little lightheaded.

Mazie dismounted first, offering to help Hope down.

"I'm good," she pushed at the lady's hand. She had this.

Krissy came bounding out of the house, a huge smile on her face that fell when they made eye contact.

"Sweetie, you okay? You're white as a ghost."

"I'm fine. I just need to go to the ladies' room. Mazie?" She glanced at the other woman.

"Oh, in the house, down the hall, and to the right."

She'd barely entered the bathroom when her friend called her name.

"What?" Hope asked, and her voice sounded odd in her own ears.

"What're you doing?"

"Going to the bathroom."

"I can see you through the crack in the door. Why is your head between your legs?" Krissy's voice was teasing, but made her feel like telling the truth.

"Trying not to pass out."

"Why are you going to pass out?" This was louder, concerned.

"I think I broke my wrist."

"How?!"

"Didn't Mazie tell you? The horse kicked me while I was trying to cut him free. He panicked when it saw a snake in the tree."

"Oh, shit! We better get you to the hospital." This time, Krissy sounded calmer.

"No. It's probably just bruised."

"Come out of there and let me look at it, at least."

When Hope obeyed, she extended her left arm to her friend. The swelling was obvious. It was turning purple around the edges.

"Yeah, you're going to the hospital," Krissy said with a motherly tone.

CHAPTER 21

They sat at the ER for over an hour, with no one acknowledging that they were waiting.

Krissy was irate. She paced. "I can't believe it's taking so long! What's wrong with these people? Can't they see you're hurt?" she fumed.

"Your pacing isn't helping," Hope teased.

"I know. I just get so frustrated. I want to help you and I can't."

"You are helping me. You're keeping me from thinking about things."

"The pain?"

"Yeah, the pain." Hope couldn't tell her it wasn't the pain in her wrist, but in her heart. She wished she could text Nick and tell him what happened. To have his voice comfort her, even though he couldn't be there.

He'd never replied after her last text.

Nothing.

Not even a goodbye.

Her name was finally called, breaking through her dark thoughts.

"Do you want me to come with you?" Krissy asked.

"No, it's all right. They'll just ask me what happened and rush me off for X-rays."

"Okay. I'll wait here for you."

"I hope so. You're my ride home," Hope threw over her shoulder before following the nurse.

When they got to the exam room, the nurse began the inquisition. "Before we do any X-rays, is there a chance you could be pregnant?"

"No—" Hope said automatically, then remembered all the sex she'd had with Nick. "I…umm…I guess it could be possible, but I'm on birth control."

"Well, there is always that one percent chance. We'll take a little blood to run to labs, just to make sure," the nurse said, patting her uninjured hand.

Her heart pounded.

She'd thought about telling Nick to get a condom but hadn't acted on it. Why not?

She was on birth control.

Because we were hot and bothered and not thinking straight.

How many times?

Too many…

Not enough…

She took a deep breath to calm herself.

It wasn't likely she could be pregnant. Her periods were never regular, so the likelihood of getting knocked up was slim, even if she hadn't been on the pill.

The nurse stepped out to gather her supplies.

She returned with news.

"But I can't be! I was on the pill!"

"Like I said, there is always that one percent. Were you on any antibiotics prior to having intercourse?"

Hope found herself blushing at the words until they sunk in.

"Oh shit! Yes. I had a sinus infection right before I took off to Los Angeles. My doctor put me on an antibiotic for two weeks. But I thought they'd proven most antibiotics didn't affect hormone treatments?"

"That is correct. But there are still a few. Do you remember what you were on?"

Hope scrunched her brows together, struggling to recall. "I don't remember.But it was something for people with an allergy to penicillin."

"That's most likely what did you in. But, congratulations."

It was about an hour before Hope returned to the lobby, and Krissy. They'd put her wrist in a brace, and gave her a ream full of paperwork.

"Well?" Her friend jumped out of her seat.

"It's fractured. I have a prescription for pain pills I gotta fill. And I need to ice it for fifteen-minute intervals."

"So you'll live?"

"I will. But I won't be getting a new horse anytime soon."

Krissy smiled. "I'm sure not."

They filled Hope's prescription and her friend took her home. "Do you want company?"

She sighed. "I appreciate it, but no. I'm gonna watch a movie and crash early. But thank you for everything you've done for me today. It means a lot."

Hope went to the kitchen and popped a bag of popcorn, then shut all the blinds. It was almost dark in the living room, even though it was midafternoon.

She put in a favorite movie, *Ever After*, and tried to get comfortable. She did her best to stay awake, but it was no use, and soon fell asleep on the couch.

𝄞𝅘𝅥𝅮𝅘𝅥𝅯

OCTOBER CAME and went without issue. Hope had little to no morning sickness, but had yet to tell anyone her situation.

She was afraid to tell her family; they were strong church members, and she would bring them shame. Even if she was a grown adult, fully capable of caring for a child when unwed.

Hope didn't tell her best friend. She feared Grace would tell Blaze, who would tell Nick. She wasn't ready for that.

Telling her bestie would come sooner, rather than later. Grace kept pushing for Hope to come for Thanksgiving. She wasn't taking no for an answer.

As the holiday loomed closer, she longed to get out of going, and assumed she might get her wish.

Her beautiful friend hadn't said a word about it in days. Hope was relieved. Until she opened her emails the weekend before Thanksgiving.

Travel arrangements stared her in the face.

Seriously?

She grabbed her cell. "What the hell, Elvis. I told you I couldn't make it!"

"And I don't believe your bullshit. You are flying down after work on Wednesday and flying back Sunday night. You won't miss any work. I know your neighbor will take care of the pets. She never minds, even if you do. So pack a bag and be ready for the car to pick you up at 6:30 p.m. Don't argue..." Her best friend went on and on.

One would never know the woman had been through hell at the hands of a so-called-friend.

Hope missed her terribly. She *wanted* to share her news. However, it wasn't something she wanted to do over the phone.

She succumbed, agreeing to come for the weekend.

Grace squealed with excitement.

Just days later, Hope stepped off the small plane at the Burbank airport. She was happy to be in the smaller airport—instead of LAX—and, closer to Grace's new home.

She'd packed light, only bringing a small carry-on, so it didn't take her long to get going. Hope put her hand on her belly; the tiny bean was still small, but she was just starting to show. She saw the bump, but would her best friend?

If not, she needed to figure out how to tell Grace.

Her bestie was waiting, just outside security.

Blaze was right beside her, holding her free hand.

The sling was gone, but Grace still had a cast on her wrist. The walking boot was gone, and a lace-up brace was in its place.

Hope had a feeling it would be awhile before Grace was back in a pair of heels.

She tugged at her oversized jacket, trying to keep her secret a little longer. She stepped into her friend's open embrace, hugging her like she never wanted to let go.

She'd missed her friend, but didn't realize how much until that moment.

When Grace let her go, she took a half step back, only to have Blaze grab her hand and give a hard squeeze.

"I'm glad you're here. My Gracie wouldn't shut up about getting you here. I think she really needed you. Thank you."

Hope didn't know what to say. It'd been a while since she had felt needed. Blaze rescued her, in a way.

"Do you have a checked bag?" he asked.

She shook her head.

"Awesome. Let's get outta here." Grace beamed.

It might be late November, but in Burbank, the temperature was still nice and warm. As soon as they were in the car, Blaze flipped the switch to fold back the top of his convertible mustang.

Hope sighed as the not-so-winter wind whipped around her. They were at Grace's place in no time. Her friend lived very close to the airport.

They pulled into the parking lot of the townhouse, but instead of parking the car, Blaze pulled up to the curb.

"Sorry I gotta drop and run, but I've got a few things to take care of before we have dinner tonight." He kissed Grace. "See you in a little while."

They climbed out and headed inside.

Her bestie proudly gave Hope the tour of her little place.

A lot had changed in terms of Grace's things. She had a new couch, kitchen table, and bedroom set. But Frisco, her pink and orange stuffed tiger, still sat on the bed.

After what had happened, Hope understood the need to change up her furniture. However, Grace's antique dining room table had been a prized possession. Whatever had happened involving the table must've been terrible.

A shiver went up Hope's spine, and she banished the dark thoughts.

Grace led her to the couch and sat, patting the spot beside her. "Now that Blaze left, do you want to tell me what's going on?"

Her friend's voice was motherly, and she couldn't help herself.

Hope took a deep breath. It seemed so much harder to say out loud. "I'm pregnant."

Grace's eyes went so wide the whites showed. She opened her mouth, but no sound came out. Until she tried again. "What? How…long have you…known?" her friend sputtered.

She held up her wrist, the wrapped brace now took place of the fiberglass cast she'd worn until a week ago. "They did a blood test to check before they did X-rays."

"You've known for weeks? Did you tell Nick?"

"No."

"No?" Grace's voice went up. An almost-yell. "How could you not tell him?"

Hope sighed, praying her friend would back off. She'd never done well with confrontation. "I wanted him to be able to walk away without feeling guilty."

Grace raised an eyebrow at her.

"I just didn't want him to feel obligated to me, or worse—blame me for doing it on purpose."

"Why would he think you did it on purpose?"

"I don't know. I was on birth control but we never talked about safe sex, even though I thought about it. I should have pushed."

"Did he ever provide a condom?"

Hope shook her head.

"Then he's as much to blame as you."

"I know, but there are thousands of women out there that would have his baby just to get his money, or even be connected in some small way for the rest of their lives. I don't want him to think I'm that kind of person."

"Nick loves you. He wouldn't think like that"

Hope snorted. "Just because he said it on national TV doesn't make it real. It was a ploy. Publicity."

"No, it wasn't. I saw his confession. Even though I was in the throws of my own excitement with Blaze's declaration, I know what I saw on Nick's face.

"An act," Hope pushed.

Grace threw her hands up. "Agree to disagree then."

Hope nodded.

"So what are you going to do?" Grace asked.

Hope shrugged. "Go home after the holiday and start getting things ready for the baby's arrival."

"Are you ever going to tell him?" she asked. "Nick needs to know. It's not right to keep a child from its father."

"If he reaches out, I will. But you have to swear not to tell Blaze."

"What? Why?" Grace sounded offended.

"Because, he'll tell Nick and I don't want him coming back because of an unplanned pregnancy. If he does return, I want it to be for me."

"Wait, what? Come back? I thought you two were keeping in

touch. Nick gave no impression you two were no longer together."

"He hasn't been dating a new girl?"

"No, why would you say that?" Grace cocked her head to one side.

Hope sighed again. It was one thing to think the words, but another to say them out loud. "He never replied when I told him I landed that day. Our goodbye kiss at the Denver airport felt so final."

"Final?" her friend frowned.

"It felt like he was telling me goodbye forever."

"You didn't try texting him again? Remind him you're still around?"

"Gracie, I shouldn't have to remind him! If he wanted me in his life, he would've responded. A text, a phone call. Something. I got nothing. But a farewell kiss. A real goodbye"

"And what if he never reaches out?"

"I have good health insurance, and I can take maternity leave. I'll convert my office into the baby's room and put my desk in the library."

"Wow, you've got this all figured out."

Hope narrowed her eyes. Grace's tone was odd; she couldn't figure out if her friend had been sarcastic or serious. Maybe a bit of both?

She got it, her best friend was now stuck between a rock and a hard place. They had been friends for more than half their lives. But she couldn't force Grace to pick sides. Only she could make the decision whether to tell Nick. She was so torn.

Would he reject them both?

Could she handle that?

She took a breath so she wouldn't sound irritated. "I've had little else to think about the past few weeks."

Grace sighed. "I don't want to fight with you, but I think you are wrong. My best friend is pregnant by my man's best friend, who I care for, so yeah. I'm torn! I want you to do the right thing here, whatever you think that is. And no matter what happens with Nick, I'm always here for you. If you need to, you can always move here. I could convert my office to a nursery. Anything you need, I'm here."

Hope laughed. She could just see herself trying to move, with three dogs and an enormous belly. "I appreciate it, but it's not necessary. Let's just see what happens."

CHAPTER 22

The next morning, Hope busied herself preparing her grandma's apple salad recipe. She tugged at her shirt, trying to lower the hem a little more.

She was only three months along, but because of her short stature; she was definitely showing. She'd found some cute garments that didn't look like maternity clothes, but there was no way she was going to hide this from Blaze. Her bestie's man was too shrewd.

He helped set everything in the dining room and took the bowl of apple salad from her hands.

Hope gritted her teeth and waited for him to return into the kitchen.

Please don't notice.

Please don't see.

Grace was at the sink, washing the potatoes she was about to put in a pot of boiling water.

Hope had strategically placed herself between the island and Blaze to hide her belly.

"So, Nick's having Thanksgiving at his mom's house. I guess

they're trying to fix their family. After everything that happened, they needed time together. It's only a few days, because we have to get back on the road. I was hoping he'd be here with you," Blaze said.

The news eased her mind. Nick wouldn't just show up, even though her heart ached to see him again.

Maybe Blaze would back off, if she revealed the truth about her and Nick.

She blew out a breath.

"He wouldn't be here with me. Even if he didn't need to be with his family."

"Why'd you say that?" There was actual concern in his voice.

"He doesn't want me." Hope looked down. Saying the words out loud made them ricochet off her heart, and shoot down her spine, followed by a stinging tingle in her limbs.

She *wanted* him to want her.

Now...she had his baby inside her, and she didn't want him back for that.

She blinked away tears. She couldn't cry now.

Stupid pregnancy hormones.

Blaze rounded the island and brought her in for a hug. "I don't know why you'd say..." He pulled her tighter, and stared her down. "What the hell is that?" He practically pushed her away, yet held on to her shoulders, looking down at her belly.

"It's a bean," she whispered.

Blaze looked over at Grace. "Why didn't you tell me?" Hurt made his voice thicker.

"I just found out last night," Grace whispered.

"So... Does Nick know?" Blaze's brows were drawn tight, and his mouth was a hard line.

"No."

"I hate to ask this, but...is it his?"

Fire flashed in Grace's eyes as her head snapped around to face her lover.

Hope's heart lifted a little that her bestie would defend her so vehemently.

"Of course it's his!" Her friend yelled at him.

Hope didn't care she hadn't had to answer for herself.

"I'm sorry, babe," he said before making eye contact with Hope again. "But why haven't you told him?"

Again, her friend spoke before she could. "Because he never came back," Grace whispered, wiping her wet hands on the hand towel that rested on her shoulder.

"What d'you mean he never came back? How could he? We had rehearsals, then hit the road. There wasn't time for him to go visit."

Hope let out the breath. "He didn't come back to me in any shape. No texts. No calls. Nothing. I sent him a text when I got home from Denver. He never replied. When he kissed me goodbye at my gate, it was…" She couldn't say it again. Her eyes clouded with tears. Stupid hormones.

Grace joined them at the island, but looked at her man instead of her. "I think she's given up on ever seeing him again."

Blaze pulled his phone from his back pocket, but Grace covered the device with her hand.

"You can't tell him," Now her friend was angry.

"What do you mean, I can't tell him? He deserves to know."

"Blaze, it's not our place—"

"Yes it is!" Blaze's voice reverberated off the kitchen walls.

Hope stepped closer. "He made his choice. He doesn't want me. I won't burden him with something he doesn't want."

"You don't know that. You can't begin to comprehend what our lifestyle is like. It may not have been his choice to not see you. When we're on tour, we're at the mercy of the promoters and upper management. We sleep and perform. And if we're lucky, we get to eat once in a while. You have to at least give him a chance to know his own kid. It's his right. And I don't even mean legally."

Hope shook her head. Her eyes burned. It hurt too much.

She'd lived one day at a time, and tried not to borrow trouble.

She hadn't noticed she was crying until Blaze reached out and gently took one tear from her cheek before his arms encircled her. Her eyes stung with more tears. "Please, don't tell him," she whispered.

Blaze groaned, as if he was really torn.

Guilt rose up and bit, but she couldn't apologize.

He finally capitulated. "I don't like it, but I won't." He pulled her into a protective hug. "But I want you to know, if you need anything, I'll be here for you."

Relief flooded her, and made her knees wobble. Hope nodded.

Blaze pulled away gently, but she couldn't meet his gaze.

He gently lifted her chin with two fingers, so she'd have to. "I just have one request."

Hope finally looked into his eyes, but she frowned.

"Can this kid call me Uncle Blaze?"

Hope laughed through her tears.

NICK WAS JUST GOING through the motions.

He loved touring. It'd been his world for most of his life. This time, he was emotionless.

He knew the choreography; never forgot a lyric.

His heart wasn't in it.

He sang to the fans, played the part, gave them the show they wanted. However, Nick couldn't tell the difference between day or night.

He didn't know where he belonged.

He felt so lost.

Help me.

The right decision was to reach out to her, get answers. He

was Nick *fucking* Ford, one of the hottest men in the music industry.

Why did she push me away?

Everything about the situation was foreign. He left women, not the other way around. He should've been over her within a few days, if not hours. For some reason, he couldn't let go.

I love her, damn it!

He couldn't let go because she was so deep inside him, wrapped around his soul, he was missing a piece of himself.

But he wasn't willing to do what he needed to get it back.

Coward.

Blaze and Grace's relationship grew more every day. He was happy for his friend.

It was the only other emotion he seemed to carry around.

Jealousy.

How did they both meet the right woman, but only Blaze got to hold on to it? Was it because of the trauma Grace had to go through? Did that bring them closer together?

No. It couldn't be.

Nick and Hope had been there for that. They carried some trauma, too. It was different, but if that was the catalyst, it would've bonded them, too.

Wouldn't it?

They'd started the tour six weeks after Denver, right on time. Beginning in Chicago with two shows the first weekend in October. He'd lost count of the number of shows they'd completed.

Blaze, on the other hand, knew exactly how many they had left until he'd get to see Grace again.

Thanksgiving week.

The tour was fifty-three shows in the U.S. and Canada, spanning over nine months. They had the week of Thanksgiving off, then six shows in December.

Then time off from the fifteenth, to the end of the month.

Sarah had mentioned a New Year's Eve event with *IHeartRadio*, and it would be filmed in L.A., but it wasn't finalized yet.

Nick would be on the road until July. It was only November.

How am I going to survive this?

One day at a time.

He sat in the living room of his home in Nashville, but he ached to be in his home gym. A chunk of his family was loitering his property. His sister, Angel, had taken over his gym and turned it into her bedroom.

Nick spent as much time working out as he did on stage. It helped keep him moving, when all he wanted to do was plop his ass on a couch, binge drink a keg, snack on unhealthy foods, and just forget about life. However, he was a popstar. Besides, working out burned, made him ache, and generally feel again. Even if it was just muscle strain.

He was trying to be happy to have his family surrounding him, but all they did was fight. He should be used to it. That was their lot in life. He'd been hoping this time it'd be different. He should've known better.

They'd just finished their big meal and were letting things settle.

He picked up his now-warm beer and took a long swig. Maybe Nick should've taken Blaze up on his offer to stay with him and Grace in Burbank.

The family was discussing, of all things, Charles, and what was going to happen with him. Because he'd crossed state lines to commit the crime of drugging Grace and holding her hostage, it could make it a federal case. Most likely they'd keep him in Denver, though.

"So, what's happening now?" his sister, and Charles' twin, asked.

"The hospital staff just medically cleared him to go to jail. Because he kept having reactions to meds, it took a lot longer to heal than they had expected," their mother explained. "We pushed his attorney to get them to keep him as long as they could, getting some physical therapy done. He can't walk yet, but at least he can stand for a moment at a time. Next comes the legal process."

Nick had tried to stay up to date with his brother's situation, but with the tour, he'd dropped the ball.

"I still don't understand," Angel pushed.

"He'll go to jail, while awaiting the outcome of the case. If his legal sanity is in question, he may go to a mental institution. Which is where I'm pushing for. My Chucky wouldn't have done this if he'd been thinking straight," Mom said.

"Seriously, Mom?" Nick exclaimed, getting up from his couch. "The kid has been messed up for a long time. This isn't something new. I saw it when we were little. If I'd been here, I could have stopped it."

His mother ignored him, turning her back to him and facing her other children. "If his mental sanity is not an issue, he'll stay in the county jail until they settle the case. It could be by either him pleading guilty or a trial."

"Does that mean he might be home for Christmas?"

Nick ran a hand through his hair, agitation rising from his gut. "Are you fucking kidding me? Do you even realize what he did? It's considered violent crimes against a person of trust. He drugged her, held her captive in her own home, assaulted her, and broke her bones! Not to mention the psychological shit he did! It's a surprise she's alive! And you want him to come home? You're all fucking crazy!" He had to get away.

Without waiting for a reply, he grabbed his car keys off the counter and headed for the garage.

Nick drove, not caring where he ended up. As long as it wasn't home. It'd been over an hour when he finally pulled into the parking lot of a park.

He wasn't wearing the best shoes for the task, but he needed to move.

As soon as he was out of the car, he ran. He ran the trails in the park so many times, he'd lost track. He finally stopped when his heart and lungs threatened to explode.

Nick headed back to the car, so he leaned his head back on the headrest and sighed.

This wasn't how he wanted his time off to go.

His phone pinged, breaking him from his thoughts. The message was from Blaze. He contemplated not reading it, but he really could use the distraction.

BLAZE: Happy Turkey Day!

NICK: Back atcha.

BLAZE: How you holding up?

NICK: Surviving. Had to get away from the family for a few minutes.

BLAZE: How's Hope?

NICK: Good, I guess.

BLAZE: You guess?

NICK: We don't talk much.

· · ·

HE DIDN'T NEED THIS, in his already stressful day. No need to jump out of the frying pan and into the fire. But…he'd play along. He had to.

No one knew she'd walked away from him.

BLAZE: Why don't we have her come to a show?

NICK: I don't know.

BLAZE: You still want to see her, don't you?

HE KNOWS SOMETHING, I can tell.
He refused to panic. Blaze was a brother to him, but this shit was none of his business, and he didn't want to talk about it.

NICK: Of course.

AND HE REALLY DID. Even if it was just to have the final goodbye talk he'd been robbed of.

BLAZE: Grace said you haven't talked to her since August.

NICK: I know. Every time I think about messaging her, something comes up.

. . .

He wasn't ready to admit what'd really happened.

BLAZE: *Find the time! Sounds like Hope's going through some stuff, and she could use some support.*

Panic hit again, but this time it was all for Hope. He wished he could go to her.

NICK: *Is she all right?*

Whether or not she wanted him, he still loved her, dammit.

Not enough to text her, though.

He ignored his own snideness, and read his buddy's latest message.

BLAZE: *Grace wouldn't say, just that she's in need.*

NICK: *I'll do my best.*

BLAZE: *I'm serious, Nick! Text her on Monday. Invite her to a show.*

NICK: *All right. Do we have one in her area?*

BLAZE: *I'll find out.*

· · ·

HE WAITED another moment to see if his buddy would continue, but nothing more came his way. Nick looked on his band's website.

Razor's Edge had a show in Tacoma. The only one in Washington. It was only two weeks away.

CHAPTER 23

"I can't believe I let Grace talk me into this," Hope said to herself as she got dressed in her hotel room just outside of Seattle.

Her bestie had set it all up, her hotel, a car to pick her up and drop her off, and a front-row seat to the Tacoma show.

Not to mention the *All-Access* Pass that would get her backstage before and after the show. Not that she'd use it before the show.

The four-hour drive had given her plenty of time to think about all the possible things that could happen at the concert.

The best and the worst.

His reaction on stage would be all she needed.

Grace had promised not to tell Nick, and had threatened Blaze with loss of limb. She didn't say which one, but Hope hoped it was his favorite part.

They all agreed it needed to be natural; Nick seeing her there.

Blaze had tried to convince Hope during Thanksgiving, that Nick was still crazy about her.

She'd argued back, citing once again their final kiss, his lack of response to her texts, and the general way he'd avoided anything that could bring her into a topic of conversation.

Now she was about to find out.

Hope located her seat, as the lights were dimming.

An enormous cloth screen hid the stage behind it. Tinkling music began as images of the two bands flashed before them. All in black and white, ten men were introduced.

Mixing images from the two bands, the crowd screamed as their favorite guy's image appeared.

Pictures of fans holding signs, the men throughout their careers.

It was a beautiful menagerie of sights.

One by one, it showed an image of the guys with their names bold in white and red print. Eddie, Nathan, Joe, William, and Raleigh, all from *Next Step*.

Then BJ, Dwaine, Scott, Thomas, and finally, Nick.

Her heart hammered with the base when his image came up.

Damn, I forgot how hot he is.

The music shifted, the notes rising to a higher pitch, bringing the crowd to a frenzy. The names of the bands began appearing, one letter at a time.

N.E.X.T.S.T.E.P.

R.A.Z.O.R.S.E.D.G.E

The music built up to a crescendo, a blast of pyrotechnics shot out sparks, and the cloth screen dropped, revealing all ten men on the stage.

They stood as far back on the stage as they could, close to the instruments, unmoving as music shifted to the first song.

It was a smooth combination of two of the band's most popular songs.

They were all dressed all in black, with various accessories to personalize each of them.

It only took a moment for the words to sink in, what song they had chosen for *Razor's Edge* part of the mash-up.

My Love.
Hope let the words fill her.

> *I'm here, my love. I'm here, my love*
> *I can take away all of your pain*
> *I'll never leave, I'll never leave*
> *You will always have me by your side*
> *I'm here, my love. I know you*
> *Your days will be filled with our light*
> *Since I'm not afraid*
> *I'll show you, That everything will be all right*

THEY SLOWLY BEGAN MOVING CLOSER to the audience.

The choreography didn't change from show to show, but Blaze was the one that stood in front of her, and somehow, it made her relax.

He gave her a big smile, like he was letting her know she was visible.

Eddie gathered all the attention, rapping the lyrics of the bridge, while the rest of the men moved to the center of the stage, where there was a runway stage that extended deep into the crowd.

They ran down the length, high fiving hands as they went.

At the end of the long stage, they all gathered together to shock the crowd when it began lifting them into the air.

The song ended with more pyrotechnics on the main stage, and the venue went dark.

When the lights slowly returned, *Razor's Edge* was gone, *Next Step* had the stage.

They performed one of their newer songs.

Hope wasn't really paying attention. She kept checking her phone to see if there was anything. A text from Blaze or Nick.

Nothing.

The lights went out again but there was activity on the main stage.

Razor's Edge was back out. Green lights and smoke filled the space where the five men stood.

The beginning notes of the song *Cheater* filled the air.

Blaze worked his way down the runway, singing the lead to the song, leaving his band members behind him, only to join them when the chorus began. By the next verse, they all were heading down the runway.

Hope's eyes were on Nick.

Look at me.

His back was by her, every time he was close enough to see her.

Had he seen her, and was pretending not to?

Was he avoiding her on purpose?

The men met at the end of the stage, breaking into an amazing choreography that finished the song.

The lights dimmed, and they disappeared.

Damn it.

By the time *Next Step* finished another song, Hope was just about done.

She chided herself to be patient.

Razor's Edge had only been on stage twice, but why hadn't he seen her yet?

Blaze had. She was plenty visible.

Razor's Edge returned, picking up where they'd left off, on the lift at the end of the runway.

Nick started off the song, but they stayed in a circle on the lift.

They turned as they sang, giving attention to the fans in that area. Singing about how she's one of a kind, she makes them get down.

Come back over here. Please.

I need you to see me.

When the song hit the bridge, they ran up the runway, getting closer to the stage, and Hope. Her heart cantered with the screaming fans, and her little bean was being rocked by the music.

She wanted to get mad at Nick.

Why wasn't he seeing her?

Hope narrowed her eyes and stared him down.

He was putting on a show, but he wasn't really in it. It didn't look like he was engaging with any fans. His brothers were reaching out to touch fans and blow kisses at the women.

Not Nick.

He was only going through the motions.

How did I miss that?

Was Blaze right?

She tried to relax and just enjoy the performance. Hope had never seen either band in concert before.

She needed to try to enjoy herself.

Don't let the night be wasted.

The next few songs, she kept her eyes off the tall blond, watching everyone else. Hope had been missing out on all those years. These bands had been around a long time. She'd always been more of a country music fan.

It was Grace who'd opened her up to new musical tastes. More of the songs were familiar than she'd assumed.

Next Step did a beautiful set of ballads, all five men dressed in suits with matching fedoras.

Hope had never wanted to be a microphone stand more in her life than she did right then.

Damn hormones.

Sure, these were some really hot men, but she'd never had

'adult' thoughts about them. Being pregnant, everything got her hot and bothered. With no avenue for release. She would've taken anyone of them right then and there.

Chill, girl!

There was a reason this joint tour was sold out. There was someone for everyone, mixed in with the ten men that made up the two bands. They were talented, hot as all hell, and they loved their fans.

She could see that with every outstretched hand, every tear that slipped down the cheeks of the surrounding women.

The hands over their hearts as they sang along, said more than any sign they could hold in the air.

Razor's Edge took the stage again, dressed all in white suits, singing a song about being lonely.

Hope felt the words deep in her soul.

She could hear it in Nick's voice, as if asking why he couldn't be with her.

Was he missing something *she* needed?

Of course, the band wasn't singing about Nick and Hope, but they might as well.

The words hit a little too close to home.

They moved forward, close to the edge of the stage, and where Hope stood.

She wasn't going to look at him, but her eyes were drawn in his direction.

Nick appeared to be on the verge of tears.

This was the first time she'd seen any emotion on his face.

He looked like he was feeling the words they were singing on a level that hurt.

It was overwhelming.

Her own eyes prickled with the telltale signs.

Can anyone else see he's hurting?

Did I do this?

They led into the bridge of the song; Dwaine took the lead,

singing to the crowd that he had nowhere to go. That *she* never gave love in return.

The song ended, and they slipped off the stage once again in the dark.

Did she want to see Nick after all?

It didn't help when they began the next song, singing about wanting to let go.

It was also the very first thing Nick had ever sang to her.

Pretending You were never here,
Stuck in a world of dreams,
Wishing I could heal my heart, All I do is scream,
Without you, I am, Unfinished.

THAT WAS how she felt now.

Hope had tried to go on like she'd never known him. Even if there hadn't been something left behind, her little bean, she'd never be able to forget him.

How was she going to face this alone?

They exited the stage, leaving her with her thoughts.

Yes, she wanted him.

Yes, he'd looked hurt.

Had she done that? Had Hope hurt him?

He had hurt her.

He'd walked away.

Blaze was wrong.

Nick wasn't still interested in her. He could've just been playing the part. He hadn't really shown any other emotions, how could she believe this concert was anything other than him putting on a show for the fans?

She sat in her seat. She wanted to leave. Hope wouldn't enjoy the rest of the show.

Next Step took the stage again, and it was time to leave.

She wasn't doing anyone, especially herself, any good by being there.

Hope really wanted to go home.

This wasn't the life for her.

Or her baby.

Two hours later, Blaze's deep voice reverberated through her as he yelled at her through the hands-free bluetooth in her car. "What the hell, Hope? Why did you leave?"

She'd called a cab to get her back to the hotel, packed her bag, and left.

Hope didn't care it was almost ten p.m., and home was a four-hour drive. She needed to get away.

"I can't do it, Blaze. I can't let him hurt me all over again."

"You didn't even give him a chance! I knew I should've given him a hint! Told him to keep an eye out. He knew you lived close to Tacoma. When I called him on Thanksgiving, I told him to invite you. Did he?"

"You called him?" Anger spiked, and she hollered back. "It wasn't your place to tell him!"

"I didn't tell him about the baby. I only said you were going through something and he should reach out to you."

"Well, he didn't." Her heart slid to her feet and tears stung her eyes for the hundredth time that night. She took a sharp breath so it wouldn't show in her voice. "So that tells me everything I need to know, I gotta go, Blaze. I'm driving. Give Grace my love."

She disconnected the call before he could say anything else.

Then she turned off her phone.

Hope didn't want any distractions while driving the mountain pass in the dark. It was December, and the road was covered in snow.

She didn't need more tears in her eyes and to crash the car.

CHAPTER 24

Tacoma had been the hardest show he'd done the entire tour to date. *She* lived close, but Nick had never reached out to her.

He was afraid of the rejection.

Could she be out there somewhere in the audience?

He was afraid to find out.

So Nick avoided all eye contact with the fans. If he didn't look, he couldn't see.

Blaze had been abnormally cheerful, and that didn't bode well for him. He'd said nothing to Nick, but it put him on guard.

Nick had done well, putting on the show the fans needed. Until halfway through the night.

One song did him in.

They sang of heartbreak, loss, and not knowing where they belonged. When he got to his solo verse, even he'd heard the break in his voice. Nick did everything he could to hold himself together.

Why was the song hitting him so hard?

He'd sang it a million times, and not once had the lyrics

affected him this way. When Dwaine took the bridge, it gave Nick a moment to pull himself together.

They had one more song before he could exit the stage.

When the concert was finally over, all he wanted to do was shower, get on the bus, and pass out in his little, dark, bunk.

Blaze came bounding over like a kid on Christmas morning.

Nick sighed inside and took a deep breath so he wouldn't say something he'd regret.

"Where ya going, Nicky?" his tattooed buddy teased.

"I'm hitting the shower. Just like you should," he said.

"Well, don't go too far. I need to show you something."

Nick shook his head. He loved Blaze; the man really was a brother to him. All the guys in the band were. He was the baby of the band, which had been hard for him in the beginning.

Going from the eldest sibling in his family, to the youngest in the band, with a gap of almost ten years between him and Scott, hadn't been easy.

He didn't need or want a big brother right then.

He just wanted sleep.

Nick slipped away to his bus while Blaze was busy chatting on the phone.

His buddy didn't look too happy, and he didn't stick around to find out what was up.

Wasn't any of his business.

BLAZE WAS in a nasty mood the following days. Whatever that phone conversation had been, it hadn't gone well.

Nick avoided his bandmate as much as possible, spending every spare minute working out.

A week later, they completed touring for the remainder of the year. The only thing left was an appearance on New Year's Eve.

He could handle that.

Grace and Blaze had invited him to spend Christmas with them.

Nick politely declined, and informed his immediate family he'd be unavailable during the holiday.

He just wanted to be alone.

No tree, no decoration, no presents.

He spent the time catching up on sleep, taking hour long showers, spending hours in his gym, and finally, beginning to write again.

It'd been so long since he'd penned new lyrics.

Everything in Nick encouraged him to pick up a bottle, but that'd been his past. He'd never let himself sink that low again.

This time, he couldn't explain it, but it truly was the lowest point in his life.

He'd never felt so lost.

Yet, there was something holding him back from complete self-annihilation. Nick needed to find another outlet. He couldn't work out all the time. He picked up his notepad and pen and let the words flow.

Refuse to exit now,
Refuse to walk 'way from it,
Refuse to clash some more,
Can we still get over it?
What 'bout what we had?
Let's get back to it

What do you need from me
What do you want to do
This is not the life,
I want for me and you

This can't continue on
Being kept apart,
These tears are still my guilt
These tears are still my guilt

THE MUSIC FILLED HIS HEAD, as the lyrics found their place on the paper. Each line hit him where he hurt.

It helped ease the pain.

Why are you still so wrapped around me?

Hope had taken him by complete surprise.

She wasn't the type of woman that would walk out of his dreams. She'd been everything he hadn't known he needed.

Nick had let her get away.

Maybe I should reach out to her?

He picked up his phone, pulled up her name, and her last text filled his eyes.

HOPE: Thank you for everything, Nick. You changed my life in such a short time. I will forever be grateful. I'll be home soon. Gonna crash hard.

HE READ IT REPEATEDLY.

Nick had been right about what she'd meant, right?

She was saying goodbye.

But…

What if she was simply saying goodnight?

Did I screw everything up?

CHRISTMAS CAME and went without further incident.

Hope avoided all calls from Blaze, even declining correspondence with Grace. She loved her best friend, but couldn't handle dealing with her and the advice she'd give.

She focused on the changes her life was about to take. She worked on building a nursery in her small home, painting the room a lovely shade of pale yellow, with a white crib and other furnishings.

Hope had been going to her doctor appointments regularly. Her midwife had given her a due day of May second.

Deep down, that math was wrong, but the midwife was convinced she was right. Hope was convinced otherwise. The baby would be born closer to the fourteenth.

The date of the baby's conception was burned in her memory, rather than the date of her cycle, which had never been regular anyway.

"Most women conceive on the fourteenth day from the start of their period. I have seen the rare case of an eighteen or twentieth day conception, but those are very few."

"I get that, but there was no chance it was prior to this date." Hope pointed on the desk calendar to the day in August when she'd first been with Nick.

She couldn't help but recall the perfect way his hard body fit behind hers as he'd shown her how to play pool. Or the delicious way he'd made her parts sing when they made love in the bathtub.

Her cheeks flushed hot when she began vibrating with need.

"It's okay, honey," the other woman said, putting her hand on Hope's. "The rush of hormones is perfectly normal. Pregnant women can have an orgasm just by thinking about a sexual encounter. I had a client once tell me she'd orgasm if she stood too close to the dryer."

Hope blushed hotter. "This is normal?"

"Completely. Now, let's look at this little one." She took a bottle and squirted gel across Hope's small, but growing belly. She rubbed a wand back on forth, ticking away on the keypad in front of the ultrasound. "Oh, look at those little fingers!" The midwife stopped and pointed to the screen.

Her heart swelled. It was one thing to hear her little bean's heart, but another to see it growing inside her.

Little fingers. Followed by little toes.

The midwife moved things around again, getting a good profile image of her baby's head.

They could see the baby's nose and mouth.

"I wonder who's nose this little one will have."

Hope didn't reply.

"Did you want to know the gender?"

Did she want to know?

"No. Let's keep that a surprise, please."

The midwife laughed. "You're not alone. A lot of parents nowadays are optioning to not find out until either a gender reveal party, or the birth."

"I never understood why people have gender reveal parties. I mean, the sex of your baby, and the gender of your baby are not the same thing," Hope said.

The woman looked at her quizzically, but didn't press.

On New Year's Eve, Hope sat on her couch, flipping back and forth between the major networks showing parties in various places, like New York's Times Square, New Orleans, and Los Angeles.

She put her hands on her growing belly, watching as *Razor's Edge* took the stage at the IHeartRadio NYE party in L.A.

Nick looked good. Rock hard. His hair had gotten longer in such a short amount of time.

Her hair didn't grow for shit.

"Maybe you'll get your daddy's hair," she whispered to her little bean.

Her time with Nick had been a dream, one that she'd never forget.

Hope rubbed her stomach, where Nick's child grew.

She could do it, raise a baby. It would be hard, but she was strong. Hope would cowgirl up and deal with it. A baby would change her life, but it would be another grand adventure.

The band finished their song, and Blaze stepped forward, grabbing the attention of the camera. "I'd like to ask my girl-friend, Gracie, to come join us for a moment."

The cameraman scanned to the side, where Grace stood, her cheeks flushed red with embarrassment.

Blaze rushed to her side and pulled her to the center of the stage, where the rest of the band was standing.

Gasps and hollers came when he dropped to one knee and reached for her hand.

He'd passed off his microphone to the closest bandmate, which was Nick.

The blond man held the mic close to Blaze so everyone could hear.

"Baby, you've brought me so much love and passion in such a brief time. But I can't imagine my life without you. I don't want to. Grace Harrison, will you do me the honor of becoming my wife?"

Hope could feel tears slipping down her face, as she watched her best friend crying, too. Her eyes darted across the screen from Grace launching herself into Blaze's arms, to Nick's face.

It was emotionless.

Except for his blue eyes.

CHAPTER 25

Nick had no idea it was coming. His best friend's proposal was a shock to them all.

He was more than shocked. It hurt him. This was something he should've known about, something he'd been a part of.

He tried to hide his disappointment from the world, not to mention his brothers around him.

The couple was congratulated, and the band left the stage to mingle with the other guest stars, as the night wound down to midnight.

The alcohol was flowing like water, but he kept plain ginger ale in his champagne glass.

10, 9, 8, 7, 6, 5, 4…

Nick heard the countdown, but wasn't really listening.

They blew the party horns; the confetti dropped from above, and people all around him were kissing.

Someone grabbed him, a robust blonde woman, stealing his breath with an unwanted kiss.

Someone else ripped him from her embrace, turned to his left, and he was kissed again by someone new.

This wasn't the first New Year's Eve where he'd been passed around like sacrificial wine at church.

In the past, it'd been a hell of a party he'd never wanted to end. Not tonight.

Not anymore.

Nick didn't want to be touched by them.

It was another's touch he craved, but couldn't have.

He didn't want to be there.

THE DAYS FOLLOWING the New Year's Eve event were spent at Blaze's place, discussing wedding plans.

They gathered in the kitchen, books, and magazines about weddings, covered the table.

"I'd sat down with Sarah a few weeks ago and tried to figure out our schedule before I popped the question. I wanted to have a date already in mind. You know how our lives are. It was hell for Dwaine and Evey to get a date in between everything going on," Blaze said.

"So, what's the date?" Nick looked back and forth between Grace and his buddy.

"Valentine's Day," she said, her cheeks flushed pink.

"Seriously?"

How cliche...

"It's the only time we could get off," Blaze said, with a bit of irritation bordering in his tone. "And, there's more," he continued. He looked over at his new fiancée, and she nodded.

Great. What could be worse than a Valentine wedding?

"We want you to be my best man."

Nick's heart skipped a beat. "Are you for real?"

"Uh, is that a yes?" Grace asked.

"Shit, yeah! I'd be honored!"

"I should tell you then, I'm gonna ask Hope to be my maid of honor. Will you be okay with that?" The sadness in Grace's voice tore at his heartstrings.

Even if he had a problem with it, Nick would've told her it was fine. He really liked this woman, and still carried a great guilt over what his little brother had done to her.

Truthfully, he was excited Hope would be there. This meant he *had* to face the music. There would be no more excuses for putting off reaching out to her.

She'd be there, in the flesh, face-to-face. It'd be worth the rejection to see her again.

"Yeah, that's cool. So what does a best man do? What can I help with?"

Grace laughed, the sound filling him with a glimmer of happiness, the first he'd felt in a while.

"Not a lot right now. You two will be back on the road soon. And Blaze was telling me something about them adding after-parties? Are you looking forward to that?"

He'd completely forgotten about that meeting. Management wanted Dwaine and Nick to host after-parties in select cities once the new year started.

No, he really hadn't been looking forward to them. It was just another part of the job.

"They'll be interesting, that's for sure. But what about you and the theater?" Nick switched subjects. "I'm assuming, as a newly-wed, you'll want to join the tour, at least after the wedding."

"I'd love to. But I'm not sure I can get away. I'll talk to Richard and Jason next week when I head back to work. Since I'm still just doing PR stuff, I'm sure I can Telework."

"When do you think you'll get back up on stage?"

She shook her head, and the flush in her cheeks faded. "Not anytime soon. I'm not ready yet. But someday."

Nick glanced at his buddy.

Blaze's scrunched eyebrows told him to shut the fuck up.

It was still a raw wound.

"Did you pick out the wedding colors yet?" Nick asked, to distract them all.

"That was easy. We have a love of the same colors."

"Let me guess… Black and red?"

"Black and red," Blaze and Grace agreed in unison.

"PLEASE STOP IGNORING ME, Hope. I really need to talk to you," Grace's voice came through the voicemail. "It's important. Call me back. If I don't hear from you in the next hour, I will keep calling, all hours of the night, until you take my call. Just make our lives easier, and *call me back!*" The last sentence was a yell.

Hope had watched Blaze propose. So the call would be about the wedding, or the news of it to come.

It'd been weeks since she'd talked to Grace. She missed her friend.

Grace was the one she always went to when she needed a pick me up, a little help, or just someone to vent to. However, between the trauma Grace had endured with Charles, and her trying to put a fresh life together, Hope didn't want to bother her friend with her own drama.

She had to remind herself, that was what friends were for. To hold her up when otherwise she'd crumble.

Hope couldn't help Grace heal from her trauma, if she didn't let Grace into her life to help her in her time of need.

She took a deep breath and called her friend back.

Grace answered on the first ring. "It's about time you answer my damned calls! What the hell is going on, Hope?"

"I love you, too," she teased. Her eyes teared up. She was so sick of crying. She silently sniffled and damned pregnancy hormones to hell, since Grace had said the words first.

"Why have you been ignoring me?"

"I've been ignoring everyone, Elvis. Don't take it personally."

"You know I hate that nickname!" Grace was upset with her, likely for being distant. She heard her friend let out a deep sigh. "I'm sorry. My outburst was uncalled for. It's just...well...I miss my friend. I've really needed you. And I'd hoped you'd need me too. Are you doing okay?"

"I'm good. Little Bean is good. Growing rapidly. My due date is May second. But we'll see what happens. I'm sorry I dropped off the face of the earth. I just needed some time to myself. But it sounds like congratulations are in order."

"You watched the New Year's event?" Grace asked.

"I did."

"Didn't he look good?"

Who's she talking about?

"Um, I guess so," Hope said, with some hesitation.

"He really needs a haircut. I keep telling him, Nicky, you're getting shaggy. But he never listens to me."

"I don't think he listens well in any form. But yeah, I was thinking the same thing. He needs a cut. Wish my hair grew that fast."

"You should see his body. Holy cow! I was doing a video chat with Blaze the other day and Nick walked behind him, without a shirt on. I've got my own man, but good God. His body is rock hard."

"Yeah, it is."

"You haven't seen him lately. I think he's working out. Like, a lot. *Oui!* Well, as much as I'd love to chat about Nick, and his hot bod, I do have a purpose for this call. My time is extremely limited, so I'll get right to it. Hope, I would be honored if you would be my maid of honor."

She'd prayed Grace would ask her; they'd been best friends long enough, it felt like a given.

But... Nick would be there.

Hope swallowed. Twice. "You realize, I'll be six months pregnant. I'm short, Grace. There's not a lot of room for Little

Bean to grow, it's all going outward. No dress will hide my belly."

Grace squealed. "Is that a yes?"

"Yes," Hope breathed out a sigh.

"Good! The wedding is in less than five weeks. There's so much to do, and I could really use your help. And I'm not worried about your belly, if you're not."

They spent the next two hours on the phone, bouncing ideas back and forth.

Hope would arrive a few days before the wedding to help finalize things. They found a dress online that would flatter her growing body.

It was red, a color she'd always loved. One of the best things about the date was the built in color choice. It didn't matter that red and black were already Grace and Blaze's favorite colors, people automatically associated red with Valentine's Day.

"We've gone over just about everything we can think of," Grace said, as the night was winding down.

Everything but one.

"We've got your dress; I think I've narrowed down mine. We picked a cake design, flowers, and the venue. Dwaine already made a claim to the music, and Thomas has the ceremony in his hands. Having five men wanting to help with this is almost over-whelming. Especially considering they are on the road and have enough to deal with."

Hope bit at her fingernails. "Gracie. He's gonna be there, isn't he?"

It was silent on the other end of the line several moments too long.

"Yes. He's Blaze's Best Man."

She closed her eyes and cringed; grateful Grace couldn't see her. Her stomach churned, and it wasn't the baby. "I guess I can't keep it a secret forever. I think we need to set something up a day or two before the wedding, to see each other. I don't want him to blow up at your wedding."

"Do you think he would?"

"I don't know. I was thinking about how Blaze took the news. He was really upset. And it wasn't *his* problem."

"Hope! Your baby is not a problem! He or she is a blessing! Don't you ever think otherwise."

"I don't."

"Good, I better let you go. The show is just about over and I need to video chat with Blaze. I'll see you in a month."

"Can't wait."

CHAPTER 26

H ope took a deep breath as she stepped off the plane at the Burbank airport.

Four weeks had flown by far too quickly.

She wanted to blame the excitement of the wedding, and all the things she was working on from a distance to help her best friend get ready for her big day.

Her dress had arrived and it fit perfectly. It was a lovely maternity gown made with chiffon. Its V-neck was flattering, showing off Hope's pregnancy-enhanced bust. It accentuated her adorable baby bump with a matching chiffon sash.

Hope felt so beautiful when she put it on.

The flight attendant took the garment bag when she'd boarded the plane, holding it in a compartment by the cockpit. They'd handed it back when she deplaned.

She didn't know what to expect when she came through the secure area of the airport.

The last time she'd been there, both Grace and Blaze had been there to meet her. *Razor's Edge* still had another five months of touring, but she hadn't looked at the show dates since her fateful trip to Tacoma.

Hope was so grateful to see *only* her best friend waiting for her.

Grace held her arms open, waiting for the much-needed physical connection.

Hope stepped into her arms and hugged her like she couldn't let go, and her little bean was a big part of that hug.

"I'm so glad you're here! I'm drowning in things to do!" Grace spoke in a rush.

"I bet! What's the first thing on the list?" she asked, ready to get this done and over.

Not that she wasn't excited to be at her best friend's wedding, but she was still completely terrified to run into Nick and the consequences of her not reaching out before now.

Her hormones had finally leveled out, allowing her to think more clearly. She knew she'd been selfish and worrying about her heart was one thing, but he did have a right to know about the baby. Nick was a good man. He might want his baby, but not her, and it was what she felt she deserved. Her guilt spoke for her.

Grace broke her from her thoughts. "I'm starving. So lunch is first! Does the baby want anything in particular?"

Hope laughed. It meant a lot that her friend was thinking about the baby first. "No, Bean is happy with just about anything. Your choice."

A short time later, they were flying down the highway in Blaze's red mustang. It was a little too cold for the top to be down, so they lowered the windows, taking advantage of a pleasant cross breeze.

"I'm gonna take you to Blaze's favorite sushi place," Grace said. "It is amazing…"

Hope put a hand on her friend's shoulder to stop her rambling. "Sweetie, um…. First, you know I hate raw fish, and second, pregnant women can't eat sushi."

"I know, silly. But they have other yummy stuff. I think you'd love their tempura dish. It's to die for."

She let her friend lead the way in.

The hostess smiled and greeted them. It was clear by her sweet expression she was familiar with Grace. "Would you like the usual today, Grace?" the waitress asked, calling her friend by name.

"I guess you come here a lot," Hope teased.

"At least once as a week," the waitress said. "Most of the time she's alone. But sometimes she brings that hot guy she's dating."

"You mean marrying," Hope asked.

"Seriously?"

"Yeah," Grace blushed a deep red. "We're getting married in..." she looked at her watch. "Less than 48 hours."

"Well, shit! That's something to celebrate! I gotta tell Lucy!" She took off without taking their order.

Hope and Grace burst into fits of giggles.

The waitress interrupted them when she returned with a tray carrying a pot of hot green tea and two cups. "'I'm so sorry, I got excited. What can I get for you?"

Grace smiled. "I'll have my usual. And Hope, did you want to try the tempura plate?"

Hope hadn't even looked over the menu, but was starving, and would eat just about anything. "It's all cooked, right? Nothing raw?"

The waitress nodded. "It's all fried in our tempura batter. It's one of our most popular dishes."

"Sounds good."

They worked their way through their meal, going over details of the wedding, what still needed to be done, and their expectations.

"The boys get here tomorrow, with very little time to spare. I'm nervous about the ceremony. I have no clue what Thomas has planned. I wrote my vows, just in case. I'll swing you by the hotel after lunch and show you where it's at. Oh, Hope, it's gonna be so beautiful! We're having the ceremony outside in the Crystal

Garden, where they are stringing peonies everywhere. Let me tell you, that was a nightmare. I couldn't get the lady to get it through her head, there was no way in hell I wanted roses at my wedding. Not in any shape or form. She kept pushing them. I hung up on her." Grace laughed. "When she called me back, I told her, rather rudely, to get it through her head there would be *no* roses, or we were taking our very expensive wedding to another venue. That shut her right up."

Hope laughed and had to blink through everything her bestie had just rambled, at top speed. "I bet it did. I can't even fathom what this wedding is costing."

"Blaze won't let me ask for the cost of things. He practically yelled at me that cost didn't matter. I'm trying to go with the flow, but it's hard sometimes."

She was glad her friend kept going on about the wedding.

They had yet to talk about what she feared most.

Would things go bad tomorrow, when Nick showed up?

GRACE HADN'T BEEN KIDDING. The hotel and its grounds were breathtaking.

The reception would be indoors, in the Rodeo Room. It had a very elegant feel to it, with an enormous chandelier in the center that reminded Hope of the one in *Titanic*.

The three rooms, Rodeo West, Center, and East, were all opened to create a sizeable room that could seat their three hundred guests.

Their wedding colors were red, black, and white. Finding decor that would work and be able to leave out red roses had been a challenge. Their design team had been up for the task.

She shared Grace's excitement to see the final result in just a few days. It was clear, besides the choice of the Beverly Hills Hotel, that the wedding was for someone with money.

It was the only time she felt like she could see them in that way. Someone with money. Blaze was just the guy marrying her best friend. She'd seen him on stage with thousands of women crying around her.

They'd been screaming for BJ. Grace was marrying Blaze.

THERE WERE two other cars parked in the driveway of Blaze's home when they arrived.

Hope looked over at Grace, when she felt the blood draining from her face.

Is he here already?

Her bestie must've seen her distress. "It's okay! That's Diane's car. Blaze's mom. I'm not sure who the other car belongs to. Let's go inside."

Hope grabbed her garment bag and Grace took the suitcase.

They didn't get too far inside, before they were greeted by a beautiful woman that could only be Blaze's mom.

He had her smile.

That smile extended past her lips to engulf her entire face. She spread her arms and pulled Hope into a big hug. "Oh, my goodness! You must be Nicky's girl! Blaze and Gracie have told me so much about you!"

She couldn't help but glare at her bestie.

Diane must've felt her tense. She stepped back, holding on to Hope's shoulders. "Don't worry, sweetie. Gracie told us about the situation. We're here for you. I can only hope it goes well, but if not, I'll bust his kneecaps."

Hope burst out laughing.

Yeah, she was going to get along with Blaze's mom just fine.

"Let's get you settled, then you can come meet the family."

Blaze's immediate family set her right at ease. His mother had a heart so big; she couldn't believe the woman offered to bash in Nick's knees if he didn't treat Hope right.

His step-father and step-sister were also quality people. Hope never would've guessed they weren't blood family, the way they talked about Blaze and each other.

It thrilled her that her bestie was marrying into this family. Grace needed a good one, since her parents had died when she was nineteen. Her bestie needed a mother figure to help her get through the challenges of married life. Most people hated their in-laws, but this would be different for her friend.

They sat around the kitchen, laughing and having a magnificent time, like they'd known each other their entire lives.

Jerry, Blaze's step-father, cracked one dad-joke after another. They'd ordered pizza to keep the fun going. No one wanted to leave or be the one to miss the fun by getting up to cook a meal.

Around ten p.m., things wound down.

They said their goodnights and headed to the guest bedrooms, when Diane pulled Hope aside and into the living room.

"Sit with me, honey." She patted the couch beside her.

Hope didn't have a chance to speak, because the woman dived right in.

"Now, I've known Nicky since he was about twelve years old. I can say I've been a mom to him on more than one occasion. Because Blaze was an only child, I was the only mom that could come on the road with them for lengthy periods of time. The other moms had siblings at home to care for. I got to know all the boys rather well. I tell you this so you understand, I know what I'm talking about."

After the evening they'd spent together, she wouldn't have questioned, even if Diane hadn't said all that.

"Nicky's a good boy. Man. He's a good man. I know he's made some bad choices in the past; they all have. Unfortunately, it comes with the band life. But that's made them who they are today. I'm proud of my boys. I can see the worry in your eyes. You have nothing to fear, but fear itself."

I can't believe she's quoting Roosevelt.

"Gracie and I thought it best we bring Nicky here, after we get them from the airport. Blaze has a beautiful backyard, with the gardens and the pool. You could sit out in the covered patio. It's serene and would be a comfortable place to reunite. We felt it should be a safe place for you both. Would that be all right?"

It lifted Hope's heart to know they cared enough about her to plan this out. She couldn't reply, the tears stung her eyes, and she was afraid if she spoke, she'd start full on sobbing.

Am I ready for this?

Doesn't matter.

It's too late now.

Hope stared at the ceiling of the room she was staying in. She'd been there before, yet found many unfamiliar design patterns in the swirls on the ceiling.

Sleep eluded her. The more she tried to relax, the more wound up she got.

Around two a.m., she crawled out of bed and headed for the kitchen.

She found Grace up, drinking something steaming from a mug.

Her best friend gave her a smile "Would you like a mug?" she whispered.

"What is it, and why are you up?"

Her bestie smiled weakly. "Just a little nightmare. That's all. And it's warm milk with a splash of honey and cinnamon."

"That would be great, thank you."

Hope waited for Grace to finish and sit before she spoke. "Do they happen often? The nightmares?"

There was a heartbeat or two before the answer.

"It depends. I have good nights and bad nights. Sometimes it's a sound that triggers it, or a scent. Not sure what brought it on tonight."

"You gonna be okay?" Guilt smacked into her, about worrying

about seeing Nick, when Grace still suffered from what Charles had done.

For a brief second, it made her worry over how Nick was doing with everything.

She was also curious about the status of his little brother, but not enough to ask Grace.

Sure, she could do an internet search, but Hope avoided looking up the Ford family at all costs.

She couldn't see Nick's face if she could help it, so she'd stayed away from the internet.

"I'll be good. Blaze has really helped me through this. And Richard and Jason. Do you remember them from the theater? Well, they're letting me work 'from home' so to speak, so I can be with Blaze for the next couple months on the road."

"That's great news!"

"Come, on," Grace said, taking their empty mugs and setting them in the sink. "We both have a really long day tomorrow."

CHAPTER 27

Nick stared at the red numbers on the clock. He'd watched them change, one by one, for the last few hours.

He couldn't sleep.

No matter how hard he tried. Even a shot of whiskey hadn't helped.

His life was going to change in less than twelve hours.

She'd either sit down and talk about what happened, accepting him for who he was.

Or Hope would crush him into a million pieces, destroying any chance they had to move forward.

Maybe there is no forward.

Maybe this is how it should be.

They both were to blame, really. Either of them could have called or texted. Yet they'd both been stubborn.

They both paid the price.

He wasn't conscious of when he'd finally stopped looking at the time and slipped into a fitful sleep, but his dreams had been filled with fear, bright colors in shades of red filling his mind.

Nick woke with a gasp, the alarm blaring, and Hope's name on his lips.

"Are you excited?" he asked Blaze as the five men in the band, and one wife, loaded into the company jet.

"Are you?" Dwaine asked, bumping Nick's shoulder with his.

"Oh, yeah," the Latin Lover's wife, Evelien, stepped up behind him. "You're gonna see the woman I heard about. The one you professed your love to, then she disappeared?"

"I thought we were going to Blaze's wedding? Not my funeral. Can we just drop it, please?" His brothers and Evey settled in their seats and Nick pulled out his earbuds.

He loved his little family, but didn't want to listen to them chatter over what they thought would happen when he and Hope reunited.

He was tired, so exhausted.

Nick prayed he'd get a little sleep. He didn't want to be a hot mess when he saw her again.

The laughter around him was too much, all before they had hit ten thousand feet. He couldn't drown them out, even when he turned his tunes up all the way.

So much for sleeping.

Someone bumped him, causing his eyes to flutter open.

"You need to join us, Nicky, have a drink," Thomas teased, handing him a champagne glass. It splashed over the rim when a bit of turbulence sent his buddy crashing into his seat. "Sorry, bro. Just take it before I spill it all over you."

Nick took the flute and downed its contents.

"I think you need another," Scott said, refilling the glass.

He had no intention of drinking at all, on what could be one of the most important days of his life.

His flute kept getting filled, and his heart was being lifted as his brothers laughed around him, excited for Blaze's wedding.

Damn, I should've eaten something.

The guys reminisced about all the crazy shit they'd done in their teen years, when everything was so new. They talked about

Dwaine and Evey's wedding, and everything that'd gone wrong there.

"I hope you don't get a stalker fan at the reception like we did. Remember that one chick, Dwaine, what was her name?"

Nick laughed. Sometimes, it wasn't a good thing if they could remember a fan's name. Most of the time it meant they were abnormally outstanding, super caring, or something outrageous to be remembered. There would always be the one that stood out, to the negative.

"I doubt that'll happen to them," Nick said, and the champagne was getting to his head. "Their stalker is already in jail." Heat filled his cheeks. He'd said it out loud. "Ah, shit. Blaze. Dude, I'm sorry. I didn't mean it like that." He set down his mostly empty flute, shaking his head in disapproval of himself. He'd had too much to drink.

"It's okay. Nothing can bring me down today," his buddy said cheerfully.

"Except maybe this plane," Thomas teased.

"You shut your mouth, boy," Scott, the eldest brother said. "Don't you dare jinx us."

"Sorry." But Thomas grinned, unrepentant.

"Well, you boys polished off five bottles of the champagne Sarah had the plane stocked with. It's no wonder you're all a little loose lipped. Get your shit together, we're landing soon," Evelien pointed out.

Nick liked Dwaine's wife.

As the first wife, she'd put up with a lot of shit from the rest of them. Soon she'd have Grace to help wrangle them.

Too bad Hope won't be one of them.

Nick looked over at the empty bottles of *Mumm Napa Brut Rose.*

How did something so girly make me so...

He couldn't say the words. Sure, he'd had drinks before, years' worth, but those bottles of champagne hit him way too hard.

All of them. They were giggling like little girls at a slumber party.

Everyone's happy.

Do I want to be happy?

Duh.

I can't get you outta my head.

Nick stayed deep in thought when the plane touched ground.

I'll make her see. She's never left my thoughts.

Whatever's keeping her from wanting to be with me, we can figure it out.

Screaming fans filled the airport lobby, just outside the secure area.

Word had obviously gotten out that BJ was getting married in L.A., and they'd come in droves to see the band exit the airport.

There'd yet to be a picture of Grace leaked to the public, which was unheard of in today's media, but that was about to change.

Blaze's mom, stepdad, and stepsister were standing toward the front of the crowd.

Jerry, his stepdad, stepped to the side, hugging up against his mom, to allow Grace to step forward.

The airport had put up rope barriers to keep the fans in line. They were doing fairly well, being respectful of each other.

When Grace ducked under the rope and headed to her love, the fans started yelling at her to get back.

Nick laughed. Maybe the other ladies would tackle Grace before she could get her hands on Blaze.

When his buddy opened his arms to take her, no one moved.

Cameras flashed.

Everyone will know who Grace is tomorrow.

He looked around, delving his vision deep into the crowd. Was Hope hiding among the masses?

When Grace took Blaze's hand and started walking toward baggage claim, his heart sank.

She didn't even have the decency to meet me here?

What's she waiting for?

He tried not to let the hurt show. Nick needed to be strong for his buddy.

No, he didn't hurt.

He was angry.

It burned red-hot in his gut, warring with the liquor flooding his veins.

His internal argument began building the moment they were in the Escalade, flying down the interstate toward Blaze's house.

Nick sat in the passenger seat, Grace and Blaze in the back. The others were in various other vehicles, rented by management.

"We're gonna stop by our place first," Grace said. "I've got to grab a few things before we go to the hotel. We need to do a rehearsal, a run through, since Thomas took over that part of the wedding, I don't know what he…"

Nick tuned her out to listen to his own demons inside arguing.

I should've called her a long time ago.

Phones go two ways. She could've texted me.

She did.

But it was goodbye.

Was it?

"Don't you think so?" Blaze said from the back.

"Uh, Yeah. Sure."

"Nicky, you weren't even listening. Don't agree unless you know what you're agreeing to. We could've been talking about shaving your head," the tattooed man teased him.

"Sorry. I was somewhere else."

"Well, get back to earth, buddy."

They pulled into the driveway of Blaze's home. Nick's heart slammed against his ribs.

Is she here?

Is she at the hotel?

Be cool.

His palms were sweating from the nerves. Would she be happy to see him? Surely, she knew he was coming. It was their best friends getting married.

She had to be there.

Another car pulled up as they were getting their luggage from the back.

Blaze's family spilled out to follow them inside.

Nick held his breath as he walked into the house. He slowly let it out when she wasn't in the kitchen.

His best friend bumped his shoulder. "Bro, you're in the southwest room. Mom and Jerry are in the floral room, and Lizzy's in the blue room."

He tried to head to the room his friend mentioned, to drop off his bag, but Grace stopped him in his tracks.

"Can I see you a minute in the kitchen?"

He set his bag there, pulled his shoulders back, and followed the chestnut-haired beauty.

Time to face the music.

Hope wasn't in the kitchen like he'd assumed.

Grace sat at the small cafe table, the one he and Blaze had had many conversions at over the years.

He'd never been more on edge sitting there before that moment.

She reached across when he sat and took one of his larger hands into her own. "It means the world to us that you're here and gonna be Blaze's Best man. You two have been through a lot. But so have Hope and I. I won't let you two ruin my big day."

"I won't—h"

She held up a hand to stop him. "I don't know what happened between you two, to cause this big riff. Neither one of you seems to want to take responsibility for what happened. But you will go out there and get your drama out of the way, so I can have a nice wedding tomorrow. Do you understand?"

Nick frowned. "She hasn't told you what happened?" Didn't girls always talk about that kind of stuff? His sisters had. So he assumed all women did.

"All she would tell me was, you don't want her."

He jumped up from his chair, knocking it backward. "That's bullshit! It's *her* that didn't want *me*! Because I'm a terrible brother, letting Charles become the monster he did!"

"You're wrong. She still loves you. It hurt her to the bone that you walked away. You never even said goodbye."

Nick wasn't having this conversation with Grace.

This was between him and Hope.

"Where the fuck is she?"

"Nick, you need to calm down. You are *not* going outside to yell at her like this in her current state." Grace's hand smacked over her mouth the moment the words slipped from her lips.

He didn't wait for her to move; he pivoted on his heels and beelined for the door to the patio.

"Nick!" Grace yelled.

He threw open the door to see Hope sitting there, on the dark tan wicker couch, her back to him.

She glanced over her shoulder, and her hazel eyes filled with tears.

He took a step forward, his anger overwhelming his senses.

A red haze filled his eyes.

It wasn't Hope he was furious with.

It was himself.

Until she stood up.

"What the fuck?" spilled from Nick's lips as he took in her round belly.

Her chest lifted with her deep breath. Then her gorgeous eyes landed on his. "We're pregnant."

Air dissipated and his lungs ached. Someone had just punched him in the chest, hadn't they?

Nick's head spun, until his brain kicked in an order to get some breaths down, so he wouldn't pass the fuck out.

Pregnant?

Pregnant!

Of all the things…

He hadn't seen *that* coming.

Nick whirled, and went back into the house, and kept walking, until he reached the front door.

He needed air.

Blaze found him on the front porch, gripping the metal rail with white knuckles.

He bent at the waist, his head hanging between his arms.

"You okay?" his friend asked.

"Why didn't you tell me?" Nick croaked, keeping his head bowed.

"Hope asked me not to. Said it wasn't my place."

He closed his eyes. That stung like betrayal, but he didn't have it in him to be pissed at Blaze. His whole body…hurt.

"Now I understand why she didn't want me." Nick looked up at his friend.

"Dude, that's your fucking baby!" The scowl on Blaze's face said as much as the tone of his words.

Nick wiped at his face. Until he felt the wetness, he hadn't been sure he was crying. He was numb. Could he feel anything? "If it's mine, why didn't she tell me sooner?" he retorted.

We're pregnant.

Hope's statement reverberated and he shoved it to the back of his mind.

"Because she was waiting for you to keep in touch." Blaze's voice was calm this time.

"What're you talking about?" Nick spat.

"Uh, you told her you loved her on national TV, and asked her to text you when she landed after our fateful trip to Denver. Then you never replied. You never reached out to her. I even hinted she was going through something, and told you to call her. But you fucking dropped the ball."

"I do love her, but it can't be mine. We haven't seen each other since..."

We're pregnant.

Her words haunted him.

"Since August?" his best friend offered. "Dude, seriously? I know you're hurt, but you just called her a slut. Get your shit together. August to February. That makes her six months along."

Nick did the mental math. "So it's really mine?"

Why the fuck did she keep it a secret?

Blaze laughed. "You think I'd be yelling at you if it wasn't?"

Nick collapsed onto one of the concrete steps on the front porch.

We're pregnant.

Should he be mad?

Happy?

What the fuck was he supposed to feel?

"Oh man, I'm gonna be a dad," he breathed. It smacked into his chest, and his vision clouded again. "What am I going to do?" Finding Blaze's dark eyes as panic threatened to overtake him.

"Well, if it was me, I'd go find the mother of my child before she makes the assumption you've walked out on her, *again*."

Nick frowned.

"She's convinced herself you don't want her or the baby, asshole."

"I've always wanted her."

Blaze crossed his arms over his chest. "Good." He blew out a breath. "But *she* doesn't think so. Go. Fix this. Or Grace will kill us both for fucking up her day."

He climbed to his feet on shaky legs, and threw his arms

around his best friend. Maybe he needed to, to steady himself, but he'd never admit it aloud.

His friend hugged him back.

"Thanks, brother." Elation washed over Nick. "Dude, I'm gonna be a dad!"

CHAPTER 28

Hope burst into tears.

This was exactly what she'd expected.

Nick not only wanted nothing to do with her, but he also didn't want their baby.

Grace opened her arms, and she stepped into them, burying her face in her best friend's shoulder.

"That went well," Blaze said, sarcastically.

"You get him, I've got her," Grace said.

"I'm so sorry, Gracie, I've ruined your wedding," Hope sobbed.

"Are you kidding me? This isn't about me, sweetie. This is about you and Little Bean. Don't worry about me. Worry about what my soon-to-be husband is gonna do to your baby daddy."

She couldn't even smile. "I'll never forget the look on his face, not for as long as I live." She hiccupped through her tears. "That's it. It's over. He rejected me just like I thought."

I'll be strong tomorrow; today I just need to fall apart.

Grace rubbed her back, trying to soothe her.

It only irritated her.

Hope just wanted to be alone.

"I'm sorry, I can't…" she pushed out of her friend's arms and took off into the enormous gardens, on the other side of the pool of Blaze's property.

Grace didn't go after her, and for that, she was grateful.

She leaned against a tall tree, trying to hold herself up, but her legs were weak and she slipped down.

Hope pulled her knees as close to her chest as she could, wrapping her arms around them, concentrating on the serenity of the scene before her.

She hissed when a sharp jab came from her stomach.

She placed my hand over the spot. When it happened again, it hit her.

This was why she had to stay strong.

Her little bean had fluttered like a butterfly for a while, but this was the first real movement she could feel from the outside.

She smiled through her tears. It was something she'd secretly been hoping would happen *after* she reunited with Nick, a first they could share together.

He'd robbed her of that, too.

"Hope?" Nick called.

At first, she'd assumed she'd dreamed his voice up, considering what she'd just experienced. Hope hated that she loved the sound of her name on his lips, and wanted to savor it.

"Hope?"

The second call confirmed it was real.

She crushed her eyes shut tighter. "Go away," she whispered, not caring if he'd heard her or not.

"No," he said.

Closer. Too close for comfort,

She opened her eyes.

He was kneeling in front of her.

His blue eyes were so intense, she had to look away.

"Go away!" Hope said louder. "I don't want you here."

"Are you saying you don't want me?"

She pushed at his shoulders, causing him to fall back on his ass, but she didn't care.

He stared at her, shock written across his face, and his eyes wide.

"You're kidding, right?" she screeched. "You left me behind, like the piece of trash I must be. Something you used, then walked away from." Hope stood, using the tree as leverage. "I did everything you asked! I messaged you when I landed. And you *never* returned the message. And that kiss at the airport? What was that?"

Nick stood too, dusting off his jeans. "That was you, telling me goodbye! I've kissed a million women, and God knows I can tell when a woman is saying goodbye or goodnight. Your kiss was as final as they get, Hope. So don't fucking blame me for this! You could have texted me anytime in the last six months. How about the day you found out? That would've been a great day to call and say, *'Nick you shithead, don't fucking ignore me, I've having your baby!'*"

She walked away, back toward the house.

She needed to leave.

Pack her bag and head to the airport.

Hope didn't need to be there.

Grace would have to get married without her.

"Hope! Don't walk away from me!"

"Why not?" she screamed back. "You walked away from me first!"

She spun on her heels and glared with all the anger and hurt she'd built up. "Like you said, you've kissed a million women, so what do you need *me* for? Go find another fat cow to warm your bed!"

"What the fuck is your problem?"

"You!" Hope took another step toward the house, but stopped in her tracks when a sharp pain filled her abdomen, and she had

to double over to breathe. Agony engulfed her form, from her back to her distended tummy.

Nick was on her in an instant, wrapping his arms around her. "Are you okay?"

She couldn't reply.

She couldn't even push him away.

The pain was so intense.

"Grace! Blaze! Somebody, help!"

Hope looked down at her feet, trying to find some air, when she saw the blood dripping into the green grass.

Oh, dear Lord, I'm bleeding.

"No," she cried. "Not my bean!"

Her heart rose in her throat. She didn't want to lose this baby. She forced herself to calm down. Panicking wouldn't help.

Diane, Blaze's mother came running out of the house.

"Where is Grace? Hope's bleeding!"

The panic in his voice caused hers to triple.

Diane got right in front of her, glancing at the blood before lifting Hope's chin to see her eyes. "Sweetie. A little blood is normal. But I think a checkup would be a good idea. I'll get Jerry. Grace and Blaze went to the hotel to do rehearsals, and said you two needed some alone time." The older woman looked at Nick. "I was under the impression from my son, this was going to be a happy reunion. All I heard was very upset voices. I don't think they would've left if they knew you two would fight. Let's go to the hospital. I'll meet you out front."

Nick was still holding Hope tight, trying to help her walk to the gate on the side of the house.

HE CONTINUED to hold on to some part of her as Jerry drove the four of them to the nearby hospital.

"I've left three messages for Blaze. I'm sure we'll hear from them soon," Diane said over her shoulder to them.

Hope was too worried about her baby. She couldn't believe Nick was beside her, crooning in her ear.

"Honey, I'm so sorry. Please forgive me. I was just so stunned by when you said—"

"It's yours," she said. "Little Bean is yours."

"I know. I don't doubt that."

She searched his face to see if he meant it.

The intense depth of his blue eyes, the red rim around them, told her he did.

They pulled into the Emergency Department and Nick was out of the car before Jerry had come to a complete stop.

He ran through the double doors and was back with a nurse and a wheelchair by the time Hope was getting out of the car.

Diane stood beside her, holding her hand to help her into the wheelchair.

"Should we come with you," Diane asked, worry finally lacing her voice.

She thought about it for a heartbeat.

"I'd rather go alone. Please." Hope glanced briefly at everyone, lingering a moment longer on Nick.

He needs time to think and process this. Without me.

"It's okay," the nurse said as she wheeled Hope through the doors, "I'll take good care of them and get back to you soon."

♪♪

NICK PACED THE WAITING ROOM, becoming more impatient by the second. His best friend and his fiancée had finally gotten the message.

Now the entire band was sitting with him, waiting to hear what was happening with his unborn child and the woman he loved.

The nurse that'd taken Hope back, opened the main door,

looked right at Nick, and smiled before waving for him to follow her.

Grace jumped up from her seat, but the nurse held up one hand.

"I'm sorry, only one at a time, and Dad goes first."

Grace nodded and sat, taking Blaze's hand.

"I'll be back with an update for the rest of you soon," she said, then led Nick through the secure door.

"Looks like you have a strong support system out there. She's lucky to have you all."

Nick glanced at her, then studied her.

She was about his age, maybe a few years older. She showed no signs of knowing who he, or who his *support system* was.

It was on the tip of his tongue to say something when they arrived at a room on the left.

"She's resting, so try not to wake her."

"Thank you," he said, slipping quietly into the room.

Hope was lying in a propped up hospital bed. Her head was angled to the side as she slept.

He stood next to the bed, mapping her face with his eyes. He took her left hand in his and ran the other through his hair.

Hope's eyes fluttered open. "Nick?"

"Shh," he said. "The nurse says you need to rest."

A tear slid down her cheek, and he wiped it away.

"I was so scared," she said, her voice wavering.

"It's gonna be okay."

There was a soft knock on the door and the doctor stepped in. "Hi, the nurse told me you were here. My name is Dr. Royster." He went to the opposite side of the bed from where Nick stood. "How are you feeling, Hope?"

"Weak," she breathed.

The doctor looked up at Nick.

"Has she filled you in about her condition?"

Nick shook his head and glanced at Hope for an explanation, his heart in his throat.

When she said nothing, he shifted his gaze back to the doctor, trying to blink away tears, but they slid down his cheek.

"I think it was brought on by stress, and too much physical activity. I recommend bed rest and that she sees her regular doctor as soon as she gets home."

"And the baby?" Nick asked, swiping a stray tear away.

"The baby's fine. A little bleeding isn't abnormal," the doctor said.

"How long do I have to stay here?" Hope asked. "I have a wedding tomorrow."

"Congratulations." The doc looked back and forth between the two of them.

Nick didn't correct him, and neither did his love.

"I think you'll be okay to return home tonight, but if you have any more bleeding, you need to return right away," Dr. Royster said. "Try to take it easy tomorrow. Sit as much as possible. Keep the dancing to a minimum. I hope the ceremony isn't too long. It's not a Catholic Mass, is it?" He chuckled but continued on. "I've given her a mild sedative to keep her calm. I'll have a prescription sent to the pharmacy. Like I said, stay off your feet as much as you can, and no crazy honeymoon. Looks like you already did that." He winked at Hope.

"So she can leave now?" Nick was eager to get her out of there and finish their conversation. In a much more civil way. Plus, he needed to update his family.

"I'll send the team in here to get her discharged. It was nice to meet you. Take care of them." He looked right at Nick.

"I love them more than my own life, sir."

The doctor slipped away, leaving them alone for a moment.

Nick didn't waste a moment. He grabbed her hand, kissing the palm, then each tip. "I lost you once, and it almost killed me."

Hope laughed. "I beg to differ. I could feel your new and

improved six-pack when you were holding me. I'd say you're more alive than ever."

If she wanted to be light-hearted, he could do that. He lifted the edge of his navy-blue T-shirt, showing her what she'd commented on. "I needed an outlet, something to throw my built-up tension at. I worked out. A lot. I hope it's okay."

Her eyes turned hungry, like she could eat him for dinner.

His balls tightened. He cleared his throat so he wouldn't get swept into arousal. "Hope, I won't lose you again. I thought you didn't want me. Who would want to be with a man that couldn't be there? I wasn't there for Chuck, and he broke. He almost killed Grace. I have to live with that guilt for the rest of my life. I know my life is crazy, and it's scary. But I think we have something worth fighting for. Even if we didn't have a little something tying us together."

Hope reached for his hand, pulling it to her belly without saying a word.

Nick felt a fluttering beneath his fingers. "We're going to be parents." He was unable to hold back his smile.

"Are you mad at me?" she whispered. Her voice was full of worry, and she wouldn't look at him.

"Why would I be mad at you?"

"Well, you're a famous popstar, and I thought you'd think I did it on purpose. Then I didn't tell you…"

"I'm pretty sure it took two of us to make this little one." Nick caressed her belly. Wonder washed over him as his child moved again, as if responding to his touch. His heart skipped. His eyes watered. "I'm sorry it's taken me so long to get here. I got so wrapped up in what I thought you thought, I never *thought* to actually reach out and find out the truth. I hope you can forgive me." He searched her hazel eyes for answers.

She crooked her finger, urging him in close.

Nick burned for what she was offering but was afraid to take it. He leaned in close, letting her make the first move.

She slipped her hands into his hair, wrapping her fingers around the long strands, giving her the access to pull him closer. Hope kissed him softly.

Once, twice.

She released him, letting him sit back down before she spoke. "I've wanted this so badly, to know I'm not alone. To know that this little one will grow up knowing it will depend on both parents." Hope placed her hand over his that still rested on her belly.

"I love you, Hope."

"I love you, too."

Finding out he was going to be a father was one thing, feeling his child move had brought him to tears, but hearing those special words slip from her cherry lips was his undoing.

CHAPTER 29

"I refuse to sit in a chair for the ceremony!" Hope yelled at Nick. "I'm fine to stand. It will only be about twenty minutes. If I get tired, I'll let you know and you can get me a chair. Fair?"

He was only trying to help, but she was getting frustrated.

After getting home from the hospital, Grace had threatened to cancel her wedding until after the baby was born to make sure Hope was safe.

All the boys in the band were on her like stink on shit.

No one would let her do anything.

Hope had put them all in their place before retreating to bed.

Nick had gotten a bit of a laugh when they'd finally retired for the night. Apparently, Blaze had told him he was sleeping in the southwest room; AKA the room *she* was already settled in.

He'd planned all along things would work out.

The guy had been beaming with satisfaction.

"Fine," Nick agreed to her stipulations. "But you will sit for the receiving line."

"Seriously?"

"You argue, you don't go. I'm not losing either of you ever again."

He'd said something of that nature more than once in the night.

"I can't believe I missed all this." His left hand rested on her belly while they spooned in bed. "Just because I was too egotistical to admit I might've been wrong. This whole time I thought it was you that didn't want me, and you thought I didn't want you? We really need to work on this whole communication thing."

"If we're gonna work on that, I'll start. *I'm* communicating to you that your bulging erection is pressing into the small of my back and making my hormones go crazy. The doc said no sex, but you're making me want to break my word to him."

Nick had chuckled, and the sound was music in her ears. "I'll communicate next." His hand slid up to cup her breast. "I thought your boobs were hot before, but damn. You got smacked by the titty fairy, didn't you? I can't wait to see them naked, again."

"Not tonight. I need sleep. Tomorrow is gonna be a long day." Hope had been glad they weren't facing each other, because she couldn't help her smile of self-satisfaction. Nick was hotter than when they'd been together before, but so was she. Even with a huge belly.

Now they were about to watch their two best friends get married.

Nick had finally given in and allowed Hope to stand for the service.

Off to the side, where the crowd couldn't see them, she waited with Grace, in her breathtakingly beautiful Vera Wang gown. Her best friend carried a bouquet of peonies, daisies, and gardenias.

Grace's father had died when she was a teen. The man that had played her father on stage, in the musical that changed her life forever,was John. He was honored to walk her down the isle.

"Here we go," Thomas said, kissing Grace's cheek before leading the way.

Hope was the only bridesmaid, but Blaze had four groomsmen; the boys in the band. Thomas, followed by Scott, then Dwaine, began the procession.

Nick stepped up to Hope, offering her the crook of his arm. "Damn. Have I told you how stunning you look in red?"

"Not yet,"

"Well, you do. And, this could be us; you know."

She cocked her head, eyeing him up and down. Her words dissolved as she took him in.

His black Armani tux fit like a glove, bringing her back to the first time she'd ever seen him, walking toward her, wearing a suit much like the one he had now, and a mask.

She'd had no idea who was behind it; not really. It'd taken six months to see the man behind the mask.

Hope loved him.

She was still pissed at him for not calling or texting. But deep in her heart, she'd loved him from the beginning, despite it all.

His words finally hit her. "What do you mean, this could be us?"

Nick didn't get to answer.

The music had shifted, and he walked her out.

When they were a few feet down the aisle, the crowd gasped signaling that Grace had come around the hedge.

Thomas had explained that morning at the wedding party breakfast, sans one bride and groom, that he'd brought in his childhood priest.

The man had baptized both him and Scott—they were cousins —and the man had counseled every one of them at some point in the band's career.

One look at him told Hope the man knew Blaze. The pure joy was written on the priest's face.

She held tight to her bestie's bouquet while Grace held tight to Blaze's hands and they recited their vows.

Hope wiped at a tear that slipped down her cheek. She made the mistake of glancing at Nick. Her heart just about exploded.

He was wiping at a tear of his own. His eyes shone brightly.

She could feel his happiness. She hoped it was for more reasons than his buddy getting hitched.

Could part of that happiness be for me and Little Bean?

Everyone was dabbing at tears by the time the service was over.

Nick was true to his word, and made Hope sit in a chair for the receiving line. He'd procured her a barstool with a back that put her at the same height she's been if standing.

One by one people came through the line, giving the couple their congratulations.

A few faces she recognized, but most she did not.

Occasionally, Nick leaned over and whispered a name and how they knew them.

There were many people in the entertainment industry.

One face she recognized immediately, although they'd never met.

Eddie, the bad boy from *Next Step*, the band *Razor's Edge* was touring with, stepped up to them, greeting the other groomsmen. "So, Nick my boy, this must be the one that broke your heart," he said in his incredibly sexy baritone voice

"Excuse me?" they asked in unison, looking at each other, then back at Eddie.

"You didn't seriously think you hid that from us, did you?"

Hope didn't see Nick's face, but the laugh coming from Eddie said everything.

"Ah, shit, man! Really? You might have had the crowd fooled, but not your friends." He extended his hand to her. "I'm Eddie Wilson, but you probably know that."

Heat flushed her cheeks.

"Eddie!" Blaze called from the other side of Grace, who was standing right next to Hope. "Come here, bro! Meet my wife!"

The bad boy's attention was pulled away from Hope, and none too soon.

The man screamed sex in everything about him.

Her little bean moved, bringing her attention away from Eddie.

Hope put her hand on her left side, where the kick had been.

Nick must've seen the movement because his hand quickly went over hers.

This caused the next few guests to make comments, congratulating them, as well as the newlyweds.

"I didn't know you were expecting, Nick," the eldest member of *Next Step* said, coming up to them. He reached out a hand to Hope. "Hi, darling. I'm Raleigh, this is my husband Harvey. It's so nice to meet you! When are you due? Looks like while we are still on tour, I'm guessing."

Nick looked at her before replying. "May. We're due in May."

"Do you know what you're having?" Harvey asked.

"A baby," Nick said.

"I'd hope so," Raleigh teased.

"I didn't want to find out the baby's sex until they are born. So we all have to wait and find out together," Hope said.

"How sweet! Well, this little one will have plenty of uncles to look after him or her. We've only got one baby in *Next Step*. William's daughter. But she hasn't been a baby since I was still in the closet."

Nick, Raleigh, and Harvey laughed at the joke, but it only confused Hope. "I'm sorry, I don't…" She didn't get to finish.

"His daughter is almost fifteen, and William's date today. I'm sure you will meet her soon."

They moved on to the bride and groom and the line continued on.

It felt like hours before the last person passed through the line.

♪♫

NICK LET out a sigh of relief. He was so ready to be done with the meet and greet and get on to better things.

"Party time!" Thomas clapped his hands together with glee.

"Not yet," Blaze interjected. "Gracie says we have group photos next."

The entire group let out a groan.

"It won't take long, guys. I'm a professional. We'll get these done in no time," the blushing bride said.

He knew better than to point out, they *all* were professionals, known for their fast and easy photoshoots.

"Let's get all the stuff with Hope in it first, so she can head inside," Grace continued, pointing to where she wanted some photos.

Nick understood she was only looking out for the wellbeing of her best friend, but Hope looked irritated. He'd already learned she didn't like to be treated differently.

She was a strong woman who would push past anything.

Even if it killed her.

They took a few shots of the entire wedding party, in a nice and appropriate fashion.

Then Blaze swept Grace into his arms; Nick grabbed Hope, bending her over to kiss the hell out of her.

He had no idea what his 'brothers' were doing, but the few people watching the session burst out laughing.

During the shots with just Grace and Hope, Nick noticed the priest was still there, having a quiet chat with Thomas and Scott.

He glanced back and forth between the two scenes, the cousins and the priest, and the bride and his woman.

His woman.

His heart confirmed how true that was.

She always had been.

Nick wanted to make sure it always stayed that way.

He slowly let out a breath and stepped up to the two women.

The photographer was bitching about something, but he tuned her out.

He had a mission and nothing would stop him.

I waited all my life for this moment, and now I know exactly what to do.

Nick got down on one knee in front of Hope. "I know we seem to do things a little backward, but you're here, I'm here, so's the priest. Our best friends are here. Marry me."

"What?" Her hazel eyes bored into him. "You're not asking me to marry you right now, are you?"

He stood, grabbing her hands. "I am. Why not? We already have the perfect background; our important people are here..."

She tugged away and held a hand up. "No."

"Awesome... what? No?" It took a moment before her single word hit him. It was a sucker punch to the gut. He had to lock his knees so he wouldn't fall over.

Hope put a hand on his cheek before leaning to kiss him softly. "Don't get me wrong, I'd love to spend the rest of my life with you, but this is our best friends' wedding day. I won't take that away from them. Besides, we just spent the last five months not knowing what was going on with each other. I think we should spend as much time getting to know each other before we fully commit."

Nick heard her words, but weren't they already there?

He put his hands on her growing belly. "I think we're already fully committed." He kissed her back, just as gently. "But I'm willing to wait, if you think right now isn't the right time."

"I do."

CHAPTER 30

"I hate you so much, Nickolas Gene Ford!" Hope screamed, squeezing his hand so hard, pain bit back and he expected to see grounded numbs where his hand had been.

"I know, baby. You can hate me today. It's all right."

She'd been in labor for almost fifteen hours and was barely halfway there.

The midwife kept coming back and checking on her, letting them know how little she'd progressed.

"Where's Grace?" Hope whimpered when another contraction had come and gone.

"She's coming. She had to stop and pick up Blaze from the airport."

After the wedding, Nick had worked hard to convince Hope, the only way to work on their relationship, was for her to quit her job, get her neighbor to care for her pets, and come on the road with him.

She'd have Grace by her side during the concerts, and him at night.

In the mornings, he'd loved waking up to her beside him for the past three months.

Being so close to her delivery, they expected the baby anytime.

So they all agreed the best thing was for Hope and Grace to stay in L.A..

The moment she'd started having contractions, she'd called him.

Of course, it'd been in the middle of a show, halfway across the country.

Nick had been on a commercial plane by eleven p.m., and in her arms before midnight.

Thank God for time zone changes.

They waited until the contractions were closer together to call Blaze.

His 'brother' had insisted on being there when he became an uncle. Nick was grateful he had such an amazing family.

God knew he was becoming more estranged from the one he'd been born into. They couldn't agree on what should or shouldn't happen with his younger brother. He loved Charles. Always would. He was his little brother.

However, was best for Chuck, and society in general, was keeping him locked up. So he left them out of this. They had no clue he was about to become a daddy.

Hope gritted her teeth as another wave came over her.

"Breathe through it, baby. You've got this."

"Shut the fuck up, Nick!" she yelled back.

He tried not to laugh, but it wouldn't have mattered.

The room was filled with laughter then.

Nick glanced over his shoulder.

Grace's expression was sheepish, as all four of his bandmates came bursting into the room.

"Damn, boy, she's gonna have your balls in a jar before this is over," Blaze teased.

"You just wait until it's your turn," Dwaine said. "Evey took forever to forgive me when our son was born. Okay, it was like six weeks, but to a man… that's forever."

Grace stepped up to his woman, putting her hand on her cheek. "How're you holding up, do you need anything?"

Hope started crying. "I need to get this kid out."

"I know. It's happening. It takes time. Do you want some ice chips?"

She nodded and Grace reached around Nick to grab the cup with a plastic spoon handle sticking out.

"I can do that." He was slightly offended she was taking away the one thing he could do to help Hope.

"I know. But you need to step out into the hall and talk with your boys."

"No, I don't—"

"Yes, you do," Grace insisted. "Now. Go."

Nick took in the slight sheen of sweat across Hope's brow. "Will you be okay if I step outside, honey?"

"I'm okay. I've got another minute or two before I want to hurt you, again. So be quick."

He still couldn't believe he was there. At a hospital, about to meet his unborn child. A gift he'd never expected.

He didn't want to leave the room.

Blaze must've sensed this, because he grabbed the back of Nick's shirt and practically dragged him from the chair and out into the hallway.

"So, I got to thinking," Thomas said the moment the door was closed. "You proposed at the wedding and she said no, right?"

"Yeah, what's your point?" Nick glared, a little irritated they'd brought him out for this.

"Why did she say no?" Thomas pushed.

"It wasn't the right time. It was their wedding," he pointed to Blaze.

"Maybe now is the right time?"

"How'd you come to that conclusion?"

Scott put a hand on the his shoulder. "We know that family means a little something different to each of us. And you've been struggling a lot lately with parts of yours. Thomas came to me and thought you might want Hope to be your family."

"Obviously," Nick snapped.

"Let me finish," the oldest boybander said, with great patience. "The hospital has a preacher or a priest. Someone that could marry you. You've got your family here. Make that baby legally yours before he or she's born. Cut the red tape from the beginning."

Nick didn't know a thing about the law when it came to such matters, but Scott's words hit him hard.

He wanted Hope for his wife.

He hadn't even thought about what would happen if they weren't married before their child was born.

"Can you go find them? The priest or whatever? I'll go talk to Hope." Nick didn't wait to hear if his brothers had things under control.

He just wanted to return to her side.

Another contraction hit, right when he reentered the room. He'd barely made it to her side when the midwife came back in.

"Let's give you a check, honey, see how things are going."

Nick couldn't watch while the woman was all up in Hope's business. He just held her hand and waited for her to finish.

"Well, things have moved along rather fast in the last thirty minutes. You jumped from three centimeters to ten dilated. And you're ninety percent effaced. You'll be pushing fairly soon. I'll get the team ready."

"Not yet, she can't start pushing yet." Nick was desperate to get the words out. "We need a little more time!"

"I'm the one pushing a watermelon through a hole the size of a lemon! What the hell do you need more time for?" Hope snapped.

Another contraction hit, and her pretty face contorted. She grabbed at the side arms of the raised bed.

Grace helped her breath through it and Nick bit his knuckles.

Maybe this isn't the right time.

But... our baby.

As she was coming down from the pain, Grace glanced at him, a raised eyebrow, along with the *'I'm gonna hurt you, if you hurt her'* look on her face. "What did the boys need you for out there? Nick." Blaze's wife bit out.

"Can I have your hands, Hope?" he asked, trying to get them out of Grace's hold.

His woman could only nod.

After taking her hands in his, Nick let out a deep breath, pushing it through pursed lips. "I've got less than thirty seconds to get this out."

"All right! Let's get this party started." The midwife returned with all sorts of people behind her.

One nurse was pushing a weird-looking glass case that made his heart drop.

"Is that for the baby?" he asked, completely forgetting what he was about to do.

"Yes." She explained what they used it for.

"But the baby's gonna be okay?" he asked.

She didn't answer, or if she did, Nick missed it.

Another contraction racked Hope and his attention was brought back by his crushed fingers.

"I need to push," Hope screamed.

"Not yet, sweetie. Almost. But not yet. Breath through it."

"Nick, I hate you!"

Nick found words and shoved them out. "Hope, I asked you once if you'd marry me, and you said not yet, the time wasn't right. It's not any better now, but I love you and I want to spend the rest of my life with you. I want our baby to legally be my child. Marry me. Right now. Before it's born." He said it all in one breath, not willing to lose the chance to get it all out before another contraction came.

"Are you fucking serious?" she screamed. "*Now?* When my vagina is up in the air for the world to… ahhhhhh!" A new contraction stole her words.

"Next one, Hope. On the next one, let's give a big push!" the midwife said.

"Oh my God, this really hurts!"

His heart stuttered, but he needed her to answer. She could call him an asshole, or a fucker, or whatever, as many times as she wanted to. "Hope, will you marry me?" Nick dared ask again.

"Yes, damn it, yes! Just get this kid… ahhhhh!"

"Hope, on the count of three you're gonna push. One, two, three, push."

The scream that came from deep in her throat had Nick feeling nauseous.

He could only imagine the agony she was in.

When the midwife was instructed her to push again, the boys came back with a priest in hand, trailing apprehensively behind them.

"That's the groom." Thomas pointed to Nick.

"Young man." The priest stepped closer but clearly avoided getting a view he'd never forget. "As I explained to your, um brothers, it takes more than a few words to perform a wedding ceremony. There's paperwork that must be filed first. It's a process."

"But you could do it for emotional and spiritual purposes, right? Under the eyes of God, it's still legit, right?"

Nick loved that Thomas held his faith close to his chest.

"Well, yes. I believe it would. But the state is what matters."

"Not today," Thomas pushed.

"Hope, are you sure you want to do this now?" Grace asked, standing on the other side of the bed, glaring a deep hole into Nick's soul.

"Yes! I want my baby to be his baby," she said right before she pushed again.

"Keep it simple," Scott said.

With one last look of apprehension, the priest pulled a Bible from his pocket and flipped through the pages until he found what he needed. "Brothers and sisters, we are gathered here today, during this joyous occasion, to unite these two..."

"Simple, Father!" Thomas pushed.

"What are their names?" he asked Thomas, who was obviously the team leader today.

"Nick and Hope."

"Under the eyes of the Lord, and before your friends and family, Nick, do you take Hope to be your wife?"

"I do!"

"AHHHHHH!" Hope screamed as she bore down one more time.

Damn, how long does it take to push out a baby?

Nick hurried back to her side, opposite Grace, although, he could feel Blaze's wife's incredulousness and a new death stare in his direction.

She was going to kill him if this didn't go right.

"Under the eyes of the Lord, and before your friends and family, Hope, do you take Nick to be your husband?"

"Yes!" she gritted out with another contraction.

"I see the head! One more big push, Hope!"

"Then by the power vested in me..."

"One more, Hope! The head is out! Did you want to see," the midwife asked Nick, while the priest continued.

He could only shake his head.

He didn't want to let go of her hand, to watch his child be born. Not to mention, Dwaine had warned him not too look. His buddy had said he'd seen her differently, whatever that meant.

"Last one! That's it."

"I now pronounce you..."

"You did it, Hope. You have a beautiful…"

"Husband and wife."

"Baby girl!"

HOPE STARED into the face of her beautiful little daughter. She had a head full of dark brown hair. Of course, that didn't mean it wouldn't fall out and grow back blonde, like her daddy. She had ten perfect fingers and ten tiny toes.

Nick dozed in the reclining chair in the corner.

She'd sent everyone else home.

Well, to their hotel rooms.

Blaze and Grace didn't have room for everyone. As it was, her bestie had turned their flowered room into a makeshift bedroom/nursery for her and the little bean, so they had a home until they were ready to return to the road with Nick.

Once the tour was over, he'd already made plans to sell his Nashville home and find them something that was theirs.

"Sweet Little Bean. You need a name," she crooned to the tiny bundle at her breast.

She hadn't been able to come up with any names that felt right.

Hope and Nick had discussed a few, but hadn't singled out one they both liked. Every time she suggested one, he would mention someone named that, or it was a fan's name.

She'd tried to explain, no matter what they named their child, there surely was a fan out there with the same name.

"My beautiful girls," Nick whispered, waking up from his brief cat nap. "How are you feeling?"

Hope smiled. Her body felt like she'd pushed a tanker truck out, or like she'd been run over by a dump truck, which had always been her favorite saying when she didn't feel good. "I'm okay," she replied.

He didn't need to know how badly she hurt. On more than one occasion, she'd suspected he was going to pass out earlier.

"Did we really get married while I was delivering?" she asked.

"We did. Thomas thought it was important."

Hope's heart swell even more.

They were all looking out for her.

"His faith is important to him. The fact that he cared enough about us, and our baby, that he hunted down a priest to marry us, means the world to me," Nick said, joining her and the baby at her bedside.

She looked down at her most precious gift. "Faith," she whispered.

"What's that?"

"Faith," Hope said louder this time. "It's something we both were missing, but carried with us at the same time."

"I guess," Nick said, looking thoughtful.

"She's our faith."

"I like that," he whispered. His smile was tender. "It feels right. Faith." He leaned down and kissed the top of her tiny head. "Our daughter, Faith."

THE END

ALSO BY ANDREA HURTT

Razor's Edge Rockstar Romance
>_Masquerade - Book 1_
>_Undone - Prequel_
>_Unmistakeable - Book 2_
>_Incomplete - Book 3_

Short Stories
>_Acting the Part in Lockdown_
>_Truth or Dare_
>_*Batteries Not Required_

Demons Within Us Series
>_Nebraska Nights - Book One_
>_Depot Dreams - Book Two_

<u>Coming Soon</u>
>**_Razor's Edge Rockstar Romance_**
>_Drowning - Book 4_
>_Inconsolable - Book 5_

The Sealgaire Saga
>_A Slice Of Hell - Book One_

Prince Cove Curse
>_Under The Sea - Book One_

SNEAK PEEK

Read on for an excerpt from
Andrea Hurtt's novella, from the *Razor's Edge* Series.

UNDONE

Now available from Piece of Pie Publishing

ORDER IT NOW

OR

GET IT FREE

Sign up for Andrea Hurtt's Newsletter
and get the ebook at no cost!

https://dl.bookfunnel.com/n9we1apx9k

UNDONE

CHAPTER ONE

"Breathe. Just breathe." Grace took a deep breath as she entered the community hall's recreational room. This was where she was going for her life-changing event?.

The lights were bright, harsh old fluorescent tube bulbs. The room smelled like a locker room.

She took in the less-than-impressive view.

The bleachers were closed and pushed up against the walls, giving the room a large cavernous feel. If anyone yelled, it would echo off the walls.

It made Grace smile.

That slice of joy only lasted a moment.

Her new costar, was about ten feet away, bouncing a red dodge ball like it was a basketball.

She cringed inside.

Those balls were made of nightmares!

"Gracie! You're here! It's about damn time! We can't get started without you. Hey! Catch!" The good looking, well-built twenty-one-year-old man threw the ball at her.

She stepped out of the way before it could collide with her. The flying red rubber hit the wall behind her only to roll back her way. Grace continued to ignore it, walking closer to not only him but the others in the room.

"Seriously, Grace. Would it really hurt that much if it hit you?" Charles crossed his bare muscled arms over his chest, looking at her with mock disapproval.

If you only knew.

She forced a smile and stood by the other actors. Grace, for all her name implied, had always been clumsy.

In middle school, they'd given her the nickname, Graceless. One time in gym class, she tried to dodge one of those red balls. She'd slipped and broke her left arm when she'd hit the wooden floor.

She'd screamed like the world had ended, and everyone had laughed. The horrible teasing was born. That was the day she lost her voice, not just physically, but emotionally. She'd become an introvert, caving in on herself.

If Grace talked with no one, no one could hurt her.

Years later, theater had helped change all that. Taking on characters, *becoming* someone else, her whole body changed.

She had poise and grace she'd never had before.

Her new addiction.

She always needed more.

"Everyone please take your seats, I don't care where. Just sit and I'll pass out the scripts," Jason, the man in charge said. He was an amazing man with a vision. At six foot, five inches, his height alone made her uncomfortable. His sun-bleached hair and copper tone shouted he spent more time outside than in a dark theater. When he smiled, and those pearly white teeth shone, it set her at ease.

Jason had been on a massive search throughout the theater communities everywhere, for actors looking to spread their wings. He needed people that could act, sing, and dance and weren't afraid to leave their homes for an extended period.

That was what'd caught her eye, and motivated her to drive the long distance to audition.

Grace took a seat next to her new costar, as she tried to push back memories she didn't need at the moment. She *had* to focus.

The script in her hand took on a permanent curved because she kept rolling it and squeezing, then unrolling and smoothing it out.

Her nerves were getting the best of her.

I still can't believe I am here. This is really happening. Mom, I'm doing it. I'm doing this for you.

The younger man bumped her shoulder, bringing her back to the moment. "Are you ready for your life to change?" he whispered in her ear, his breath warm from his earlier exertion with the damned red ball.

Andrea Hurtt is an emerging author of various romance categories. She enjoys writing a little bit of everything.

Andrea has been a dental assistant, a stay-at-home mom, owned her own clothing store, was a clothing designer with a vintage-inspired clothing line, Amaryllis Designs, even won Omaha Fashion Week for Top Designer in her category, and Top Boutique for Cancer Survivor Night.

During COVID, she wrote four novels, and an award-winning TV pilot screenplay, and moved to Vancouver, BC to pursue acting.

Andrea currently spends her days either writing books or

making #EmotionalSupportPillows and traveling around the USA with the cast and fans of the CW TV show Supernatural.

She is the mother of two children, a cat and a dog, and is a proud Army wife; residing in a haunted Victorian mansion in the Midwest.

For more books and updates:
    www.pieceofpiepublishing.com
    www.facebook.com/andreahurttauthor
    www.Twitter.com/atomicbombshel1
    www.Instagram.com/AndreaHurttAuthor
    www.Amazon.com/author/andreahurtt
    www./tiktok.com/andreahurttauthor